His grip was too strong . . .

the surface of his palm too hard when he reached out and helped her to her feet. The subtle potency of his hands as they tightened on hers sent a charge through her system, warning her how close she was to being lost. Rebecca tried to conjure up her first meetings with Dan, with his stupid doll and his stupider jokes, but all she could think of was that his hands felt good on her. Much too good.

She hadn't just warmed to him. She'd grown overheated. It was definitely time to leave.

"We've got to do this again sometime," he said, his voice gravelly with innuendo.

"Talk, you mean?" she asked.

His eyes sought hers, dark with desire and a clear warning. "Talk dirty."

Dear Reader,

Ah, those sweet days of summer! Long, hot days . . . and even hotter nights. . . . Judith Arnold evokes all those wonderful feelings of a summer love here in *Opposing Camps,* this month's Calendar of Romance title.

There's nothing like the passion and excitement of falling in love during special times of the year— times that will forever have a special place in your memory. That's the magic you'll find in A Calendar of Romance.

Next month, Tracy Hughes brings you an extra surprise in September's Calendar of Romance title—#455 *Sand Man.* Don't miss it!

We hope you're enjoying all the books in A Calendar of Romance. We'd love to hear from you!

Debra Matteucci
Senior Editor & Editorial Coordinator
Harlequin Books
300 E. 42nd St., 6th floor
New York, NY 10017

JUDITH ARNOLD

OPPOSING CAMPS

Harlequin Books

TORONTO • NEW YORK • LONDON
AMSTERDAM • PARIS • SYDNEY • HAMBURG
STOCKHOLM • ATHENS • TOKYO • MILAN
MADRID • WARSAW • BUDAPEST • AUCKLAND

Published August 1992

ISBN 0-373-16449-1

OPPOSING CAMPS

Chapter One

A lone canoe glided across Silver Lake, silent except for the muted slosh of the paddle breaking through the still surface of the water. Above the lake the sky shimmered with stars and a fragile sliver of moon. Around the lake the forest loomed. The leaves of oak, maple and ash trees whispered in the balmy summer breeze, regal firs permeated the air with their crisp scent and ferns fluttered and undulated just inches above the ground.

Glancing at the black lace underwear, the coiled rope and the folded plastic on the floor of the boat, Daniel Macklin grinned.

Ahead of him on the western shore he spotted the freshly painted swimming dock of Camp Chippewa. He paddled the canoe past the groomed strip of sandy beach, past a second dock to the pebbly coast at the northern limit of Chippewa's shoreline.

He loved when Silver Lake was like this, placid and dark and all his. In only a few hours the girls of Camp Chippewa and the boys of his own Camp Mohawk would descend upon the lake's western and eastern shores, and for the next seven and a half weeks peace would be only a distant memory.

Despite the red bandanna he'd tied Indian-style around his head, the wind blew tangles into his hair. He hadn't been to a barber since early May, and now his straight brown locks were long enough to cover his collar in back. In his faded and battered jeans and his loose-fitting green T-shirt, with Camp Mohawk emblazoned across it in angular white letters, he looked like a refugee from a hippie commune.

He stroked his paddle in a wide arc, steering the prow toward the shore. Chuck's cabin stood apart from the center of Camp Chippewa, nestled into an isolated clearing in the forest. Dan was delighted by the secluded location; he didn't want any of the camp staff to hear him skulking around the grounds now.

As he glided into the shallows, the pebbly lake bottom scraped against the bottom of the canoe. He climbed out, splashing through the water in his canvas sneakers, and dragged the boat the last few feet to the shore. He paused and listened. It was maybe an hour before dawn; no sound emerged, either from Chuck's cabin or from the staff quarters in the center of the camp. Only the chirps of a few tired crickets and the hushed rippling of the water disturbed the tranquil air.

Dan drew in a long, bracing breath and smiled.

Every year he and Chuck tried to get each other before opening day. Three days before their respective summer camps opened for business, they and their staffs arrived for orientation. Dan worked harder during those hectic three days than during the following seven-plus weeks; he and Chuck had a standing agreement not to contact each other then.

At least, not in a civilized way. They'd established a ritual of precamp skirmishing, though, inaugurating every summer with a practical joke of some sort. Three years ago Chuck had strung about a mile of Christmas tinsel between the mess hall and the shower house at Camp Mohawk. Two years ago Dan had broken into Camp Chippewa's canteen, removed all the candy bars in stock and left in their place boxes of dried prunes. Last year, on the eve of opening day, Chuck had replaced the rustically carved wooden Camp Mohawk sign with a Camp Schmohawk sign.

The boys who spent their summers at Camp Mohawk prided themselves on being "Hawks"—tough, intrepid braves who could outswim, out-boat, out-race and out-camp the prissy-sissy girls of Chippewa. Dan had been lucky to discover the counterfeit sign before the campers started arriving. They would not have taken kindly to being called schmoes.

Personally Dan had thought Chuck's stunt was hilarious. But he'd felt obliged to shake his fist indignantly at Chuck and warn, "I'm gonna get you next year!"

Now next year was here, and Dan was about to fulfill that promise.

He grabbed everything from the canoe, then stole up the narrow path to Chuck's cabin. The windows were dark but open; the curtains fluttered in the breeze that entered through the screens.

Ducking down behind the bushes, Dan went to work. Within minutes he'd strung up between two trees an inflatable doll, her arms spread wide, dressed in sheer lace underwear with a sign around her neck: I Survived Camp Chippewa—Barely.

Satisfied with his work, he turned and started back toward the lake—and froze when he found himself staring into the beady black eyes of a skunk.

The skunk stared back.

Dan groaned inwardly. He had to get past the animal to reach the canoe and make his escape—without getting sprayed.

He took a slow, cautious step toward the skunk. The skunk remained immobile, staring at him, twitching its nose. If only Dan had some food, he could use it to lure the skunk off the narrow footpath to the lake.

Chuck would have food. One corner of the single-room cabin was fixed up as a kitchenette. Even if the refrigerator was empty, the cabinet would be well stocked with munchies. Chuck was devoted to junk food.

All Dan had to do was sneak into the cabin and grab a bag of taco chips—without waking Chuck.

He gazed forlornly at the skunk. The skunk twitched its nose again. It certainly didn't seem inclined to move.

Dan scoured the ground around him for something small. He found an acorn and tossed it at the skunk. It only stopped twitching its nose and started twitching its tail.

Dan swore under his breath, then tiptoed to the cabin's door, praying Chuck was sleeping soundly. The skunk watched Dan's stealthy movements, its tail rising and falling ominously and its eyes glinting with malevolence. Swallowing, Dan closed his hand around the doorknob and twisted.

It was locked. Still, the noise jolted the skunk, who flinched and sprang toward the trees.

The noise also jolted someone else. "Who's there?" came a woman's voice from inside the cabin.

Dan reflexively dived for cover, darting across the clearing and hunkering down behind a fallen log near the inflatable doll. Only when he was reasonably well hidden did the truth register on him.

There was a woman in Chuck's cabin.

And she was not Chuck's wife.

Irene would make several day trips from Long Island to visit Chuck each summer, but she would never, ever spend a night among the snakes or the mosquitoes, the spiders, those adorably twitchy skunks and the other assorted vermin that shared this corner of the Catskill Mountains with camps Chippewa and Mohawk.

Despite Irene's squeamishness regarding the lower species, Chuck adored his wife—or at least claimed he did. He vehemently defended the institution of marriage, boasted about his own sixteen years of connubial bliss and never passed up an opportunity to tweak Dan on his single status.

So why was there a woman in his cabin at 4:30 a.m.?

The windows filled with light. At the one closest to Dan, the curtains parted and he saw a backlit silhouette. No doubt about it—it was a woman.

"Who's out there?" she shouted.

Dan didn't know whether to laugh or scowl. It was peculiar enough that Chuck was entertaining a woman in his cabin—but why was he sending her out to fight his battle for him?

"Come on," she called. "I heard you. I know you're out there. If this is some counselor pulling a prank... I swear, I'll have you fired before you know what hit you."

Dan grinned in spite of himself. Chuck had chosen a real spitfire for his little infidelity. As Dan's vision adjusted, he amended that appraisal: a spitfire with a spectacular figure. He couldn't make out her face, but the light behind her filtered through her gauzy summer nightgown to display an outline of enchanting curves.

"Chuck, you devil, you," he mouthed.

Her eyes must have adapted to the dark enough for her to spot the scantily clad doll suspended across the path, because she let out a shriek. Then she vanished from the window, leaving the curtains trembling in her wake. In an instant the cabin door was flung back and the woman stormed out into the clearing. Pulling on a terry-cloth bathrobe and brandishing a flashlight, she marched toward the doll, ran the light up and down its plastic contours and uttered a distinctly unladylike word.

Dan pondered the woman from his hiding place behind the log. The robe she wore concealed her torso but exposed gracefully shaped calves and small, delicate-looking feet. Her sleep-tousled hair appeared to be blond, and her face—what little he could see of it in the deflected light of her flashlight—was pretty, her lips full, her nose straight and her eyes wide set.

Looks weren't everything, though. They certainly weren't as important as a good sense of humor. If Chuck was going to have an extramarital affair, he ought to have found someone who could laugh at a joke.

"Where are you?" she yelled into the forest, aiming her flashlight this way and that. "Come on out! Come out and show your face—unless you're too scared to deal with a real woman. Is that it? You can only deal with blow-up dolls?"

Nobody accused Daniel Macklin of being scared of women. He rose from his crouched position, climbed over the moldering log and stepped into the clearing. "Lighten up, will you?"

Angling her head, she took in the six-foot-tall stranger invading the tiny glade and fell back a step. Her free hand automatically pinched the lapels of her robe together below her throat, and her other hand directed the beam of her flashlight from his wet sneakers up his jeans to his tooled leather belt, to his T-shirt and finally to his face. The bright glare momentarily blinded him; he squinted and shielded his eyes.

"Who are you?" The rage in her voice mixed with other emotions, fear and curiosity among them.

"Dan Macklin," he said. "Chuck could have told you. Where is the bum, anyway?" he asked, gazing past her at the cabin.

She continued to aim the flashlight at his face, irritating the hell out of him. He ducked his head, but she refocused the beam, once again blinding him. "Mr. DeVore," she said after a long pause, "isn't here."

"Where is he?"

"He's home."

"Camp starts tomorrow. How can he be home?"

She lowered the flashlight to Dan's chest, to his Camp Mohawk shirt. Just as his eyes began to stop hurting, she raised the beam back to his face. "He had a heart attack."

"What?" Dan forgot about the inflatable doll, Camp Schmohawk, tinsel and prunes and all the rest. He felt a shock of pain inside his own ribs, part empathy and part grief. "Is he all right? What happened? Why didn't anyone tell me?"

"Who *are* you?" she asked again. She kept her damned flashlight pointed at him as if he were a suspect under interrogation in some rat-infested Third World prison.

"I told you. I'm Daniel Macklin," he said impatiently. "Director of Camp Mohawk, across the lake. Chuck is my friend." Hearing his voice crack, he dropped down to sit on a granite boulder. He felt dizzy all of a sudden. Chuck. A heart attack. It didn't seem possible.

He took several deep breaths to steady himself. The woman said nothing.

"When did it happen?" he asked.

"Two weeks ago," she said, at last lowering her flashlight.

"Is he in the hospital?"

"Not anymore. As I understand it, it was a mild attack. He's going to be all right."

"Then why isn't he here?"

"He's supposed to take it easy for the summer. Doctor's orders."

Dan peered up at her. The light from the windows slanted across her face, illuminating it enough for him to see that she wasn't merely pretty. She was beautiful. Her eyes were pale—he couldn't discern the exact color, but he could tell they were light. Her cheeks arched daintily. Her chin had an appealing roundness to it, although there wasn't an ounce of fat on it—or on any part of her, as far as he could determine.

Under other circumstances he would be trying to find out more about her, testing the waters, flirting. But not now. "Two weeks ago, you said?"

"Yes. According to Mr. Birnbaum, he's going to be fine." Artie Birnbaum was Camp Chippewa's owner.

"So... what's the situation here?" Dan asked, eyeing the woman warily. "You're running Chippewa this summer?"

"That's right."

"Then we ought to get acquainted."

"I'm not so sure of that," she muttered, turning her flashlight's beam toward the doll, allowing the light to linger on the tawdry black brassiere. The doll's anatomy cried out for more air, its breasts had leaked, becoming small and saggy.

An explanation was definitely in order. Dan stood, shaped an ingratiating smile and extended his right hand. "Daniel Macklin," he introduced himself for the third time. "Chuck and I go back about four years. It's become an annual tradition for us to try to nail each other before camp begins. He got me last year. This year it was my turn.''

She moved across the clearing to the doll, her lips pressed together in obvious distaste. Then she pointed the flashlight at Dan again. ''Thank heavens Mr. DeVore wasn't here. Hearing you scratching around the cabin almost gave *me* a heart attack.''

Not Chuck, Dan thought. Chuck would have doubled over with laughter and invited Dan in for a beer. But the thought of his forty-five-year-old friend weak and pale and convalescing sucked all the humor out of Dan. He strode to the doll, unlashed the ropes that held it up and pulled the plug. It hissed and shriveled into a wrinkled heap of plastic and lace.

The snooty scowl on the woman's face made Dan wish he could find her plug and pull it, too. It didn't matter that she was gorgeous, that all she had on was a nightgown and a robe, that she was going to be living across the lake from him all summer, scheduling intercamp events with him, helping him to chaperon the weekly Mohawk-Chippewa socials. Dan wanted to deflate her.

Maintaining a civil demeanor, he said, ''Look, we're going to be neighbors through the end of August. If you don't tell me your name, it's going to be awfully hard for us to coordinate activities on the lake.''

She gave him a long, distrustful look, then relented. ''Rebecca Pruitt.''

The name suited her. Anyone who could purse her lips so primly deserved to be called Pruitt.

"Well," he said, forcing his tone to remain neutral, "I don't know how much you know about the way things are done here—"

"One thing I know," she interrupted, "is that as the director of Camp Chippewa, *I'll* determine the way things are done here. As for the way things are done *there—*" she gestured vaguely toward the lake, in the direction of Camp Mohawk "—that's your business. I have an excellent staff in place. They'll fill me in on any particulars I need to know."

He tried to guess what she did in real life. He tried to guess where she came from, what her background was, how she'd wound up with such a humongous chip on her shoulder.

"The first particular you need to know," he said quietly, gathering up his paraphernalia, "is that a sense of humor goes a long way in these parts. Good night, Ms. Pruitt." With a smile that was just this side of contemptuous, he tipped an imaginary hat at her and sauntered in long, surefooted strides down the narrow dirt trail to the pebbly beach where he'd left his canoe.

He told himself he'd won the first scuffle of the summer. He told himself that Rebecca Pruitt simply had a prickly temperament, that she was insecure about her position at the helm of a camp she knew nothing about. He told himself that at worst, he'd spend a lonely summer wishing Chuck were present to pal around with after hours.

But as he shoved off in the canoe, poling through the shallows until the boat drifted far enough into the lake for him to paddle, something deep inside him ar-

gued that the worst could be a whole lot worse than
merely wishing Chuck were at Silver Lake. A woman
like Rebecca, with her sylphlike build, her fair color-
ing and her slender legs, filled the mind of a healthy,
heterosexual man with dreams of summer love—but
her personality left that same man with the irrefut-
able impression that he'd get a warmer reception from
the limp plastic doll lying crumpled at the bottom of
the canoe.

The worst that could happen, Dan acknowledged
grimly, would be that he would find himself obsessed
with the new director of Camp Chippewa and that
he'd spend the entire summer trying to get closer to
her, only to be rebuffed.

And that would be pretty damned bad.

SHE REALLY HAD TO GET some more sleep. The coming day was going to be hectic enough, what with one
hundred fifty excited eight- to fourteen-year-old girls
invading Camp Chippewa. Rebecca desperately
needed her rest.

But she lay awake in bed, staring into the shadows
and listening to the breeze sweep through the cabin's
open windows. She lay awake, trying to focus on the
million and one things that would occupy her after the
sun rose: the final pep talk she'd have to give the staff,
the extraspecial cleanup of the grounds she would de-
mand, the charm and reassurance with which she
would greet the campers and their parents, who had
received word scarcely a week ago that some stranger

named Rebecca Pruitt would be running the camp this summer instead of familiar, beloved Chuck DeVore.

She should be sound asleep, replenishing her stores of energy. But she couldn't sleep when her mind was filled with thoughts of Daniel Macklin.

What an insufferable man. Sneaking around her cabin at four-thirty in the morning—and that disgusting doll. With the obscene undies. And that dreadful pun: "I *barely* survived..."

Daniel Macklin was obviously a jackass.

So why couldn't she stop picturing his luminous eyes with their seductively lazy lids? Why did she keep visualizing his long brown hair, his lean chest and arms, his hips, his hawklike nose and his hard jaw and his eyes again, clear and bright in spite of the hour and the darkness, sparkling with laughter and anger, horror at the news of his friend's illness, and something else, some other emotion that was either disdain or desire or a mixture of the two?

Forget it. If he disdained her, fine, and if he desired her, tough luck to him. She wasn't available.

She'd had her own reasons for accepting Artie Birnbaum's frantic plea for assistance in running Camp Chippewa that summer. Artie's daughter was a student at the Claremont School, where Rebecca was the dean of students, and when Artie had learned of his camp director's heart attack he'd phoned the school and asked the headmistress if she could recommend anyone who might be suited for the job. Rebecca had been ideally suited—not only was she a dean at an all-girls' school, but she'd also had experience teaching Outward Bound courses in Maine and fifth grade on the Cherokee reservation in North Carolina. She knew kids and she knew camping.

Artie's job offer couldn't have come at a better time. She needed to escape for a while, to put some distance between herself and her life in the city, to avoid her family's disappointment and reassure herself that breaking up with Wallace had been the right thing to do.

Wallace was a charming man, well-bred, sophisticated, intelligent, professionally accomplished—everything that was supposed to matter when one was a Pruitt. Rebecca was twenty-nine, about to cross the invisible demarcation separating marriageable women from desperate ones. Wallace claimed to love her.

Except for those few small character traits he wanted her to change. Like her passion for the great outdoors, her enthusiasm for camping and backpacking, her independence. Her rebelliousness. Her stubbornness. Her competitive streak. Her thickheaded, mule-headed insistence on proving how strong and self-sufficient she was.

Just a few minor adjustments.

She'd tried, but she hadn't been able to shape herself into the proper Pruitt daughter everyone wanted her to be. So she'd broken the engagement and fled for the mountains. And here she was.

Living across the lake from a creep who thought life-size anatomically correct female dolls were funny.

Forget the doll, she told herself. Forget the man.

Rolling over, she punched her pillow into a new shape and sank down, waiting for the ancient springs of her mattress to stop whining. Tomorrow, she resolved, she would talk to Chuck DeVore. Chuck had offered his help, "Anything you need to know, Rebecca, just call me."

She hoped one of the things he could do was offer some words of wisdom about how to endure a summer with someone as infuriating—and as infuriatingly sexy—as Daniel Macklin on the loose at Silver Lake.

Chapter Two

"Retaliate," said Chuck.

Rebecca stared through the open window at the whirlwind of activity outside. It was one-thirty, the afternoon sun was high and bright, and girls—in Camp Chippewa polo shirts and white sailor hats— swarmed the bunkhouses, lugging backpacks, bags of cookies and huge stuffed animals.

Rebecca thought of all the vital chores she had to attend to, but after shaking well over a hundred hands and reciting "Welcome to Camp Chippewa!" more times than she could count, she'd ducked into her office and called Chuck DeVore. "Last night some clown named Daniel Macklin came over from Camp Mohawk and pulled an outrageous practical joke. What's going on?"

Chuck had laughed and said, "If Dan got you, the best thing to do is retaliate."

"What do you mean?"

"Let me tell you about Dan," Chuck said. Rebecca smiled; telling her about Dan was exactly what she wanted him to do. "Danny Macklin," he declared, "can be pretty frisky when he wants to be, but he's the greatest guy in the world."

Sure, Rebecca thought wryly. Who else but the greatest guy in the world would harass a woman at four-thirty in the morning? Who else but the greatest guy in the world would think a doll wearing black lace unmentionables was amusing?

"'Frisky' is an understatement," she muttered. "Unless you mean frisk in terms of frisking people. Do you know what he did? He snuck over to Chippewa before dawn and woke me up, and—"

"Okay, look, I'm sure that whatever he did last night was intended for me, not you. But listen, Rebecca—you've got to go with the flow. Don't take it so seriously. It's summertime. Have fun with Dan."

Logically Rebecca understood that by "fun" Chuck was referring to nonsense like the previous night's caper. However, another, less rational part of her brain interpreted Chuck's advice in a much different way. She envisioned Dan Macklin's dazzling eyes, his athletic physique, his wild hair, his thin, sensuous lips.... His goofy sense of humor. His genuine distress at the news of Chuck's illness. The way his gaze had lingered on her bare legs and her throat and her mouth...

She wasn't going to have "fun" with him, not like that. Absolutely not.

As to the other kind of fun... Though it wasn't really her style, she supposed she could be as frisky as Dan Macklin. If that was how things were done at Silver Lake, she'd give as well as she got.

"What else can you tell me about him?" she asked. Her interest wasn't the least bit personal, she assured herself. She was asking only because she believed the more she knew about him, the better her chance of outsmarting him.

"During the winter he's a high school English teacher in Pleasant Valley, over in Westchester County. He loves working with kids, and I keep telling him he ought to get married and have a few of his own. He says he plans to once he grows up."

Which might be in a few centuries, Rebecca fumed silently.

"His idea of a gourmet meal is pizza and beer, although given his druthers he'd prefer to eat something cooked over an open fire. He's a real whiz when it comes to camping skills. Also a terrific swimmer. He can swim across Silver Lake from Camp Mohawk's dock to Camp Chippewa's and back again in under an hour and not be out of breath. The Hawks adore him."

"The Hawks?"

"That's what the boys of Camp Mohawk call themselves."

"I see." She curled her lip at the macho pretensions of the nickname. "Do the girls of Camp Chippewa have a name I ought to know about?"

"Dan calls them Chippies," Chuck said helpfully.

Rebecca grimaced. "Why doesn't that surprise me?"

"Listen, he's a terrific guy," Chuck insisted. "Get to know him. You two could have a good time together."

Again that small, irrational part of her mind rose up like a river after a downpour, flooding her with notions about what a good time with Dan Macklin might entail. She was saved from her thoughts by a timely rap on her office door. It swung open, and Maggie Tyrell—college senior, Chippewa alumna and Rebecca's second-in-command—appeared. "Rebecca? We could use you down at the waterfront, if you're not too busy."

She gave Maggie a quick nod. Into the phone she said, "Chuck, I've got to run. How are you feeling?"

"Bored."

"That's a good sign. I'll talk to you later."

"Okay. Take care of those Chippewas for me."

"Don't worry about it."

"And take care of Danny, too."

Her smile took on a glint of vengeance. "I most certainly will," she promised.

CHUCK'S LINE WAS BUSY.

Dan would have liked nothing better than to remain in his office, dialing the number again and again until he got through to his old buddy. He'd spent the morning greeting incoming Hawks and their parents, and sorting out crises all over the camp. At last, at around one-thirty, he'd had a chance to escape the bustle for a few minutes. He'd called Chuck, wanting to find out what he knew about the alluring new director of Camp Chippewa.

He slammed the phone down, raked his hands through his disheveled hair, did a brief drum solo on his desk with his index fingers and then dialed again. Still busy.

One of the senior-boys' counselors materialized in the open doorway with a camper in tow. The boy was tall and stringy in build—probably about thirteen or fourteen, Dan calculated, the age when puberty ran about a year behind height—and handsome despite his music-video style of grooming. He had a few freckles; his hair had precise double ridges razored into it above each temple. He wore baggy flowered shorts and a loop of leather around his neck.

"Hi," Dan said, shunting aside all thoughts of that damnable woman across the lake and giving the camper a beaming smile. "Who have we here?"

"This is Adam Kember," the counselor answered. "We're having a little problem."

Dan swiveled his chair away from his desk and studied Adam intently, never allowing his smile to lose its wattage. "A little problem, huh."

"I'm going home," Adam said.

Dan digested this news with a sage nod. He continued to scrutinize the boy, who looked neither distraught nor pugnacious.

"You are indeed going home," Dan confirmed. "August 28."

"No," Adam asserted in a reasonable tone. "I'm going home *now.*"

Again Dan adopted his wise-elder look. "Well, Adam, that's going to be a real problem. Truth to tell, pal, I don't think we can arrange it."

"His parents have already left," the counselor added.

"I guess they want you to stay here at Mohawk," Dan said.

"Who cares? I'm going home," the boy insisted.

"I hear what you're saying," Dan said, extending his hands palms up in a helpless gesture of commiseration. "I just don't know how we can accommodate you at this point. I hate to say it, Adam, but you're kind of stuck."

"I am not," Adam said in his eerily calm voice. "I can leave."

"No can do. See, there are contracts and insurance companies and all kinds of messy stuff that'll come crashing in on us if you try to leave. It's not like Camp Mohawk's a prison or anything, but we can't just let you walk out the gate. If we did, it would go down really bad. So," Dan continued when he sensed Adam was about to speak, "the deal is, we're just going to have to make your time here at Mohawk so awesome you're not going to mind staying. I mean, that's the way I see this thing happening. I know where you're coming from, and so does Pete—" he waved toward the counselor "—and, hey, we'll all work on it together. How does that sound?"

Adam blinked. "I'm going home."

Dan exchanged a quick, impatient look with Pete, who shrugged. "Do you want to tell me what's bothering you about Camp Mohawk?" Dan asked Adam.

"This place sucks," Adam said bluntly.

"Well, that certainly sums it up," Dan muttered. He offered a sympathetic smile. "Do you like swimming? Boating?"

"My folks belong to a *rilly* neat yacht club in Mamaroneck. Why should I be stuck in some leaky rowboat on your puny little lake when I could be at the club, checking out the babes?"

Dan resisted the urge to criticize the boy's arrogance. Given what Camp Mohawk cost, nearly all the campers came from middle- and upper-class families. They had the financial wherewithal to be snobs.

"Did you know," Dan said, "that there are a whole bunch of babes spending the summer right across our puny little lake?"

Adam lifted his left eyebrow. "Yeah?" he asked, trying hard not to appear interested.

"That's not to say we spend every waking minute fixated on the young ladies of Camp Chippewa, but we're certainly aware of them, and I think that if you keep things in perspective you might wind up having a much better summer here at Mohawk than you realize. Why don't you give it a try, pal?"

Adam meditated for a moment. His gaze drifted toward the window, through the sparse woods to the shimmering blue expanse of the lake. Obviously he was imagining what lay on the other side of that lake.

Babes, Dan thought with an indulgent grin. Girls for the precocious Mr. Kember, college-age counselors for Pete and his brethren and a woman for Dan, if last night's chicanery hadn't spoiled his chances—and if Rebecca Pruitt underwent a personality change.

"I don't know," Adam said slowly. "Maybe I'll stay till the first social."

"Good enough. You stay till then, and then we'll check in with each other and see how it's going. Okay?"

Adam left the office with his counselor. Two seconds later Pete poked his head back into Dan's office. "His trunk was half-filled with *Playboy* magazines," he whispered.

"I'll tell the cook to add a little saltpeter to his chow," Dan whispered back. Pete rolled his eyes, then grinned and disappeared down the hall.

Dan rotated his chair to face the window. He stared out at the lake, just as Adam had done, and tried to visualize the ladies, young and slightly older, of Camp Chippewa. One lady's face came immediately into his mind's eye. What was that nonsense he'd told Adam about how the citizens of Camp Mohawk didn't spend every waking minute fixated on the females in residence along Silver Lake's western shore?

REBECCA GRIPPED the chrome ladder and hauled herself up onto the raft. She wiped the water out of her eyes and slicked her hair back from her face.

The sky had lost nearly all its light, but a warm orange glow arose from the embers of the stone-rimmed campfire pit on the beach where Chippewa's first-night powwow had taken place earlier. A few counselors and maintenance men lingered around the smoldering pyre, drinking soda and talking softly.

Rebecca stretched out on the gently rocking raft, using her folded arms to cushion her head, and listened to the muted chatter and laughter on the shore. The mild wind caressed her back.

With all the campers in their bunks, her time truly belonged to her. She could relax, drift off, let herself be lulled by the soothing motions of the raft beneath her.

She was on the verge of dozing when an unnervingly familiar voice invaded her drowsy mind: "Hi, there." Lifting her head, she found herself face-to-face with Daniel Macklin.

He was seated in an aluminum canoe, his hand curled tightly around the rope that anchored the raft to the dock. Although the sky was shadowed in dusk, she could see more of him now than she'd seen last night.

That was unfortunate, she acknowledged, because the more she saw of him, the more difficult it was to deny how handsome he was. She admired the lean symmetry of his face, his bright greenish blue eyes sparkling beneath seductively lowered lids, his nose as strong and sharp as his chin, his mouth spread in a beguiling grin. She directed her attention to the glossy mane of hair that tumbled loose and straight to his shoulders, and then to the sinewy strength of his arms, the golden skin overlaid with pale brown hair. The rest of him was out of her line of vision—which was probably just as well.

"How did your first day go?" he asked when she failed to return his greeting.

She couldn't be so blatantly rude to the man Chuck DeVore had described as the greatest guy in the world. On the other hand, she saw no reason to be particularly friendly toward him. Actually she *did* see a reason—several reasons, in fact, starting with his thick brown hair and working her way down. . . .

Plenty of reasons, but not good ones.

Giving him an aloof smile, she said, "It was pretty tiring. I suppose it would have been easier if I'd gotten a full night's sleep last night." Her pointed gaze left him no room to misconstrue her words.

He only chuckled. "Treat me nice, and I'll let you sleep tonight."

Privately she acknowledged that the longer she stared into his beautiful eyes, the more likely he *wouldn't* let her sleep tonight. She would spend the night tossing and turning, haunted by his alluring good looks.

Her gaze strayed once again to his strong hands, his virile chest, his lean, masculine thighs. "I can't imagine ever wanting to treat you nicely," she said, her even tone disguising her uneasiness.

He laughed. "How's the water?"

"Why don't you jump in and see for yourself?"

"Great idea," he played along. "Of course, I'd have to get undressed first. Do you think you could stand it?"

"Barely," she replied, punning.

He smiled at her use of his joke from last night. "Here's a better idea," he suggested. "I'll strip if you will."

"I'm as stripped as you'll ever see me," she retorted. His thorough inspection of her in her modest maillot made her regret her words. She felt his gaze on her legs, on the shadow of cleavage visible above the scooped neckline. His imagination stripped her without shame or subtlety.

"You shouldn't swim alone at night," he reproached, although his smile remained.

"I'm not alone. There are some staffers on the beach."

He glanced toward the shore, frowning slightly as he attempted to identify the people lounging near the campfire. "Hey, is that Maggie Tyrell? Maggie!" he shouted, releasing the rope and swinging his paddle back into the water.

Rebecca glanced over her shoulder at the beach. The embers had nearly died, and in the descending gloom the people looked like dark phantoms. One female phantom stood and faced the water. Rebecca recognized the outline of Maggie's curly hair and knee-length shorts.

"Dan?" Maggie shouted, starting toward the dock. "Danny Macklin?" Maggie picked up speed as Dan paddled toward her. They arrived at the edge of the dock at the same time. "Danny! You old fool! How are you?"

Dan rose slightly in the boat as Maggie knelt down. They embraced and showered each other with affectionate insults. To her surprise—and dismay—Rebecca suffered a pang of jealousy.

She couldn't be jealous, she reproached herself. She ought to be relieved that Maggie was an old friend of Dan's. Maybe Maggie would be the butt of all his practical jokes from now on, and he'd leave Rebecca alone.

She did her best to tune out the counterpoint of their voices as they caught up on a year's worth of news and banter. Burying her face in her arms, she tried to let the raft's motions once again soothe her nerves. But she couldn't deafen herself to the effervescent music of their conversation and then the lapping of the paddle as Dan boated back toward her.

"Boy, it's great to see her," he said as he glided alongside the raft and grabbed the rope. "I've known Maggie Tyrell since she was a sixteen-year-old clerk. Now look at her—going into her senior year at Penn State. It makes me feel kind of old."

Rebecca almost blurted out that he *was* kind of old to be flirting with a college student. He was a high school teacher, for God's sake.

Then again, he hadn't really been flirting. Rebecca was just overtired and overwrought. She'd misread his affection toward Maggie because she was in a weird mood.

Why she was in a weird mood was a question she preferred not to answer, especially when Dan was so close to her she could smell his clean male scent, so close she could feel his breath along the edge of her arm.

"I'm glad you and Maggie are friends," she said in her deceptively complacent voice. "You and she can work out all the details of those intercamp activities you mentioned."

"You mean, like the first social? I'll have my assistant set it up with her."

"Ah. Then we directors won't even have to be bothered." She focused her vision on a tree in the distance beyond his left shoulder so she wouldn't have to look into his eyes. The darker the sky got, the bluer they appeared.

"We just have to be there."

Startled, she frowned at him. "We do?"

"Of course. We have to set the tone."

"What tone?"

"The tone of coed affability."

"Coed affability?" She laughed in spite of herself, then bit her lip when she saw the way her laughter softened his gaze.

"We're there to make sure the kids get the hang of it." He smiled. "I've never danced with Chuck, but I can dance with you."

"Forget it."

"Don't think I *want* to dance with you," he said with an exaggerated show of panic. "I'm thinking only of setting a good example for the campers."

"Then don't bring an inflatable doll to this thing."

He grinned. "I mean, we want to make sure the Hawks and the Chippies don't view each other as archenemies. We want them to treat each other with respect, so you and I will have to treat each other with respect."

"Hmm." She mulled over his advice. "Well," she finally granted, "I suppose I could *pretend* to respect you."

His smile didn't flag as his gaze intensified on her. "I'll bet you're real good at pretending," he murmured, his voice low and insinuating.

She bristled slightly. "What's that supposed to mean?"

"Oh, you know..." His grin widened, all dimples and mischief.

"No, I don't know." She could guess, but she deliberately feigned ignorance, curious to see how far he'd go in explaining it to her.

He opted for safety. "Pretending you have no sense of humor," he said. "Pretending you're all stone and ice inside. Pretending you think this summer-camp stuff is very serious business. Pretending," he concluded, "you'd rather not tear up the dance floor with the manly men of Camp Mohawk."

"'Manly men'?" She hooted. "An English teacher ought to avoid redundancies."

"How do you know I'm an English teacher?"

She bit her lip. "Maggie told me."

His smile took on an overconfident glimmer. "Yeah, sure."

Rebecca considered defending herself, then decided against it. "All right, then," she challenged him. "How do I know you're an English teacher?"

"You called Chuck DeVore and grilled him about me."

"I did not grill him!" she argued. "You must have called him, too, if you know I called."

"I wanted to find out how he was feeling," said Dan.

Now it was her turn to view him with incredulity. "And Chuck just happened to mention, out of the blue, that I called him."

"That's right."

"I don't suppose he happened to mention anything else about me," she half asked.

"Well, he did say something about your having been a finalist in the Miss Nude New York pageant last year, and some juicy stuff about your deviant fondness for bananas. But I didn't believe him."

One part of her wanted to laugh. Another, larger part was dignified enough to make her blush. "Did he tell you I have a fiancé back in New York?" she snapped just to shut Dan up.

It worked. For several seconds he simply gaped at her. "A fiancé? As in, some guy you're going to marry?"

"That's right," she said, although her voice faltered. She wasn't good at lying, and she didn't enjoy it. All she wanted was for Dan to back off.

"Well," he said, then fell silent for another long moment. "My condolences to the both of you."

She might have countered that marriage was a joyful thing and he didn't have to be so snide about it. She might have pointed out that his cynical remark was a sign of typical male immaturity. Instead, she said, "It isn't exactly a *formal* engagement."

Idiot, her brain scolded her. The only way to get out of a lie was to disown it, not to hedge and fudge. Yet she couldn't bring herself to tell him the truth: that her engagement was in fact not informal but defunct.

His smile returned, stronger than before. "I'm not exactly a *formal* guy," he said, lowering his paddle into the water. "I'll see you at the social."

She made a face, altogether disgusted with herself. "If I decide to attend."

"You've got to attend," he declared. "Don't worry, Rebecca—it's not exactly a *formal* dance."

She dipped her hand into the lake and flung a palm full of water at him. "Go away."

He laughed and pushed off from the raft, sending his canoe out into the lake. "You should have won the Miss Nude New York pageant," he called as he swept the paddle across the lake's surface to turn the boat around. "I bet you had the most *formal* little rear end."

"I hope you drown!" she shouted after him.

"Dream on, Rebecca," he hollered with a laugh, his voice drifting over the water to her. "Dream on."

ENGAGED! Hooked, pinned, betrothed.

Spoken for.

Taken.

Why hadn't Chuck told him?

The sky continued to lose color, throwing the crescent moon and the scattered stars into stark relief. The boat drifted, its bow turning toward Silver Lake's northern shore, which climbed in a steep, heavily wooded incline. At the top of the incline was a field strewn with blueberry bushes. Dan often hiked around the lake and up the hill on his day off, pitched his lightweight pup tent on the bluff, feasted on berries and reveled in the panoramic view of the lake below him.

All that day, whenever he permitted himself to dwell on Rebecca, he had imagined himself hiking with her up to the bluff. He'd imagined that over the long summer weeks they would grow to become friends, more than friends, and that they'd schedule the same days off and hike the hill together. They would lie on a blanket underneath the stars and feed each other berries, and he would kiss the sweet purple juice from her lips, and maybe from other parts of her body....

When it came to fixations, he could get pretty inspired.

Now he'd simply have to channel his inspiration in a different direction.

He plowed the paddle through the water once more. Maybe he couldn't have Rebecca Pruitt—but he could still get her. He'd get her, but good.

Chapter Three

"I don't think I can do it," Rebecca muttered, her teeth clenched in concentration.

She, Maggie and Lisa Rubin from the kitchen staff huddled around a picnic table near the beach. Maggie had brought Lisa to Rebecca's attention at breakfast that morning. "She knows a cute little trick you might want to learn," Maggie had whispered over the platter of scrambled eggs.

Now, during the Friday-morning junior-girls' swim, Lisa was attempting to teach Rebecca her cute little trick, which entailed filling a glass with water, holding an index card firmly against the rim, flipping the glass upside down, setting it on a table and sliding the index card out from under. The water remained inside the glass—until someone lifted it, of course.

"If you really want to get the Schmohawks," Maggie explained as Rebecca picked gingerly at the corner of the index card pinned under the glass she'd overturned, "all you've got to do is leave a few of these around their dining room tonight. Tomorrow morning the kids will show up for breakfast, lift the glasses and spill water all over the place."

"Schmohawks?" Rebecca laughed, then took a deep breath and tugged the index card, jostling the glass just enough for all the water to spill out. "Damn. Ten times and I still can't get it right," she lamented. "I don't think I can do it." She eyed Lisa hopefully. "Would you like to come to Mohawk with me and the senior girls tonight?"

Lisa frowned. "Well . . ."

"How long would it take you to do?" Maggie inquired.

"Well, first I've got to break into their dining room—"

"No sweat," Maggie interjected. "I'll ask Ryan Gossens to leave the dining-room door unlocked. He's a friend of mine, and he loves a good joke as much as anybody."

Rebecca gave Maggie a dubious look. "Are you sure he won't tip Dan Macklin off?"

Maggie grinned. "Ryan is the best. We can trust him." She and Rebecca turned simultaneously to Lisa.

"What if I get caught?"

"I'll make sure you don't," Maggie promised. "Ryan will be your guardian angel."

Lisa considered for a moment longer. "All right," she said, her eyes gleaming with anticipation. "Count me in."

THE BARN, as Mohawk's recreation building was called, had been strung with balloons and streamers. Picnic tables covered with bowls of pretzels and pop-

corn lined the walls and on the platform stage stood
two old but functional stereo speakers wired to an
equally old but functional turntable. Jimmy Angelini, the boating instructor, sat on the edge of the
stage, sorting through the camp's library of anti-
quated 45s.

Surveying the scene from the doorway, Dan had to
admit the barn looked good.

"When do the babes get here?"

He spun around to find Adam Kember behind him.
Adam had moussed his hair into spikes, and he
smelled rather too strongly of some musky cologne.
Dan deduced from the clotted nick on Adam's chin
that he'd shaved, although he was clearly several years
away from having to.

Dan checked his watch. "Any minute," he pre-
dicted. "Where's the rest of your bunk?"

"Gargling. I had to explain to those weenies that
bad breath doesn't cut it."

"What would they do without you?" Dan joked
wryly. He himself had showered, shampooed, shaved
without nicking himself, gargled and donned a fresh
shirt and his newest blue jeans, just in case.

Just in case what? Chippewa's head babe decided to
send a smile his way?

Chippewa's *engaged* head babe, he reminded himself.

He had received confirmation from Maggie Tyrell
yesterday that Rebecca would be among the Chippewa staffers chaperoning the social that evening. It
probably would have been better for Dan's emotional
equilibrium if Maggie had accompanied the girls from
Chippewa, but Maggie had told him that Rebecca was

adamant about attending the social herself. "It's her first Hawk-Chippie social," Maggie had explained. "She wants to see what these things are like."

Very sensible, Dan concluded. Yet he couldn't stifle the thought—the hope—that maybe she'd decided to come because she wanted to see him.

To drown him, he recollected, his brain echoing with the last words she'd ever spoken to him.

Her last words to Chuck were quite different.

"Either she's got a crush on you," Chuck had informed him during their telephone conversation that afternoon, "or she wants you dead."

"The latter," Dan had said.

"I wouldn't bet on it. If she really hated your guts, why would she care what color your eyes were?"

Dan's mood had brightened. "She asked you what color my eyes are?"

"She said she's never really seen you in the light, and she can't tell whether they're green or blue. I told her I'd never paid much attention one way or the other, and she said she wasn't going to pay any attention, either, which, if you ask me, is a crock. She also wanted to know a little about your background."

"Probably so she can blackmail me," Dan had grumbled, although there wasn't much in his background worth paying anyone to keep quiet about.

"She wanted to know," Chuck had continued, "whether you'd ever been in trouble with the law."

"Oh, no!" Dan had wailed with fake panic. "You didn't tell her about those folks I mowed down with an Uzi, did you?"

"No," Chuck had played along. "I didn't even tell her about your arrest for robbing the campers of their canteen money. I told her you were a good boy."

"Not that any of it matters," Dan had said, his spirit sagging once more. "She's engaged."

"Is she? I didn't know that. As I recall, she listed her father as her next of kin on the insurance forms."

"Well, it's not a formal engagement."

"Then it's not an engagement," Chuck had argued. "An engagement is by definition a formal thing, isn't it?"

"Listen, pal, if you're trying to set something up between her and me, don't bother," Dan had warned him. "I'm not interested. She's snooty and stuck-up. Much too blonde. And flat chested. I've seen her in a bathing suit." And wished to high heaven he hadn't. He found himself reminiscing more often than was healthy about the way she'd looked stretched out on the raft, her hair slicked back and her skin dewy, her swimsuit clinging faithfully to every curve and indentation of her torso. Her chest was just the right size, perfectly proportioned to her slim waist and sleek hips. And even when wet, her hair was a beautiful color.

"Flat chested," Chuck had repeated sarcastically. "Ah, Danny-boy, you always know what's important, don't you."

"So, how are you feeling?" Dan had asked, anxious to clear all thoughts of Rebecca from his mind.

"Lousy. Irene bought me a treadmill. I'm supposed to walk five miles a day on it. It's killing me."

"No, Chuck—it's saving you. Give Irene a big kiss. That's the most loving thing she's ever given you, and you know it."

"Yeah," Chuck had grunted. "I know it."

The most loving thing Rebecca had ever given Dan was a handful of water in his face, he reflected as he turned to check out the barn one last time. He wondered why she had been questioning Chuck about his background—to say nothing of his eye color. Was it because she took a genuine interest in him? Or was it simply that she wanted to know her enemy?

The sound of the Chippewa bus rumbling down the lake road reined in his thoughts. He gave Adam a friendly cuff on the shoulder, then ambled with him down the path to the main entry. A score of senior boys emerged from the shower house all at once, shuffling and nudging each other as the bus pulled to a stop near the administration building.

In summers past, Dan used to march right up to the bus, welcome the girls and trade wisecracks with Chuck before shepherding the young lovelies to the barn. Today he held back, striking an artificially casual pose as he leaned against the sturdy elm in front of the administration building, his hands in his pockets and his gaze fastened to the bus's door.

He honestly didn't want to care. He didn't want to be looking forward to another encounter with Rebecca. He didn't want to be curious about how she would appear in real clothes, groomed and neat, bright eyed and wide-awake....

And *engaged*, he reminded himself.

He spotted Adam loitering against the elm tree on the other side of the dirt path, his hands in his pockets and his posture uncannily similar to Dan's. Who was imitating whom? Dan wondered irately. When all was said and done, Dan felt uncomfortably like a fourteen-year-old boy with overactive glands and mood swings to match.

The bus door folded open and a Chippewa counselor emerged, followed by a decorous stream of Chippies, all of them dressed in clean white Chippewa shirts. The last person to climb down from the bus was Rebecca.

Her Camp Chippewa shirt looked spectacular on her, he thought disconsolately. She was most definitely not flat chested.

He shaped a cordial smile and sauntered to the edge of the path, nodding and waving as the girls trooped past him to the barn. As the last few stragglers went by, he turned his smile to Rebecca. Her shirt, he noted, was tucked into stylishly pleated khaki culottes that ended a couple of inches above her knees. Her legs were a golden tan, long and slender. On her feet she had absurdly dainty red leather sandals.

His heart lurched. For God's sake, an engaged woman shouldn't be marching around in red sandals like a temptress.

Furious with her for being so bewitching—and with himself for being so bewitched—he lifted his gaze to her face. Her hair was definitely too blond, falling in a golden sheet past her shoulders. Her eyelids were dusted with a pale gray shadow, her cheeks were highlighted with a trace of blusher, her lips were shiny with gloss and she looked unforgivably pretty.

"Dressed to kill, aren't we," he said. He'd intended to sound mocking, but his tone came out plaintive.

She smiled sweetly at him. "I don't think I'm going to kill anyone," she said.

"Oh?" He did his best to adopt her light attitude. "I thought you wanted me to drown. What happened to my death sentence?"

"It's been commuted for the time being." Still smiling, she scanned her surroundings, then focused on the building at the end of the dirt path, with its peaked roof and barn-style double doors. "I take it that's where the social is going to be?" she half asked.

Her benign disposition took some getting used to. Maybe she was just trying to set a good example for her campers, or maybe she truly didn't hate Dan as much today as she had the past couple of times they'd seen each other. She *had* grilled Chuck about the color of Dan's eyes, hadn't she?

Allowing himself a tiny smile, he said, "Would you like a quick tour of the camp?"

"Maybe later." She glanced around once more before starting along the path to the barn. "We should probably get things rolling with the dance."

"Okay," he said, falling into step next to her.

"Is that the dining room?" she asked, pointing to the sprawling one-story structure to their left.

"The administration building."

She studied its log-cabin facade, then surveyed the other buildings. "Which one's the dining room?"

"Over there." He pointed out another log-cabin-style building overlooking the lake. "How come you want to see the dining room?" he asked. "Are you hungry?"

"Just curious," she said. "Mohawk is so different from Chippewa."

"You're into whitewashed clapboard architecture over there," he remarked. "We go for the log-cabin-look here."

"Logs are so much more appropriate for manly men," she declared solemnly. The twinkle in her eyes let him know she was teasing him.

"You bet they are," he agreed, pleased by her playful attitude. "None of that virginal white for us Hawks. What's with the shirts, anyway? Chuck never had the girls get themselves up in their Chippewa shirts for a social."

"It was an executive decision," she explained. "A few of the counselors expressed concern about the outfits some of the girls were planning to wear. We thought the best way to deal with it would be to issue a universal edict—everyone has to wear her official camp shirt."

"How sensible. Chuck would never have thought of that."

"Did the girls wear tarty clothing to the socials when he ran the camp?"

Dan shrugged. "I don't know. I'm sure the boys noticed what they were wearing, but—" he shrugged "—let's face it, they're kids. I didn't pay that much attention."

"Of course you didn't," she said, a hint of sarcasm infiltrating her voice. "Teenage girls aren't anywhere near as eye-catching as inflatable dolls."

Either he could get defensive about her taunting or he could laugh it off. He laughed. "Hey, look, if the girls had worn black lace underwear and nothing else, I might have paid attention."

"Such discriminating taste," Rebecca commented.

"Well, you know men," he deadpanned. "It doesn't matter whether we're dealing with latex or flesh and blood, as long as the underwear is sheer."

"You probably prefer latex," she said. "It doesn't talk back."

"That's true. And I've known too many flesh-and-blood types who are full of hot air."

At last he got a laugh out of her. It was short and subdued but real. He felt oddly triumphant.

Shoving his hands back into his pockets, he gazed at her. Her eyes met his, and she held his stare for several long seconds.

"What?" he asked.

Her cheeks darkened slightly, and she directed her attention to the open barn doors, through which the babble of voices spilled into the balmy evening air. "Nothing."

"You were looking at my eyes."

Her face flushed even darker. She pursed her lips and took a deep breath before responding. "I was just trying to figure out what color they were. Every time I see you, they seem to be a different color."

"They change," he told her.

She turned back to him, too intrigued to hide her embarrassment. "What do you mean, they change?"

"My eyes change color. Sometimes they're green, sometimes gray, sometimes kind of bluish."

"Do you wear contact lenses?"

"No. It's just a natural thing. They reflect what I'm wearing, or my surroundings. Right now they're probably green."

"They are," she said, peering boldly into them.

Her eyes, he saw, were a silvery gray. They appeared warm and inviting, like Silver Lake on a sultry, muggy August day before the heat gave way to a thunderstorm. He imagined that if the pressure changed and the climate held just the right charge, her eyes would flash with lightning.

God, but she was beautiful. Gazing down into her eyes, he imagined himself plunging into the lake, naked and alone, and letting its crystalline water swallow him. He wanted to plunge into her, to feel her all around him.

He abruptly broke from her and stepped inside the barn, annoyed that she had such an effect on him. "Let's get this dance on its feet," he mumbled.

As he'd expected, the campers were lined up along the walls, the girls on one side studying the boys warily, and the boys on the other wolfing down pretzels and nudging each other awkwardly. By the stage Jimmy had a record on the turntable and was speaking into a microphone.

"Now, I'm sure all you Hawks want to make sure the Chippewa gals feel welcome here," he began.

"Gals?" Rebecca whispered. "What a hideous word."

"It's a manly word," Dan retorted.

She rolled her eyes, then grew solemn, searching the room for her staffers. Each time she spotted one she gave a slight nod.

"Come on, guys, let's make our guests feel welcome," Jimmy shouted before starting the record.

It was a golden oldie by the Rolling Stones, and most of the campers reacted predictably, groaning and wrinkling their noses at what they considered a prehistoric song. Dan didn't care. He considered it his mission as an educator to expose teenagers to *real* rock and roll, the music that had provided the soundtrack for his coming of age.

Not surprisingly the dance floor remained empty. One brave boy dared to breach the no-man's-land at the center of the room, venturing over to the girls' side with his shoulders thrown back and his face wearing a look of confidence that bordered on arrogance. Adam Kember.

Smiling at the boy's audacity, Dan watched as Adam approached an attractive dark-haired girl. Several of her friends instantly gathered around, as if hoping he might favor them with his attention. But he zeroed in on the dark-haired one, planting himself directly in front of her, speaking only to her. If he asked her to dance, she must have declined, since she and Adam didn't gravitate back toward the dance floor. He remained before her, his head cocked slightly and his mouth twisted into a reasonable facsimile of a James Dean sneer.

Way to go, Adam, Dan thought with amusement.

"Who is that boy?" Rebecca asked.

"His name is Adam Kember. He's kind of precocious."

"Kind of? He looks as if he'd like to light two cigarettes and hand her one."

"Who's the girl?"

"Stephanie Glynn."

"Is she well versed in pregnancy prevention?"

Rebecca gave Dan a sharp look. "If your boy can't control himself, you'd better put him on a leash. I won't have him molesting my girls."

"Yes, Mother," Dan singsonged. "Hey, I do the best I can, okay? I just thought you should know that he packed a year's worth of girlie magazines in his trunk."

"Terrific," she muttered, stalking across the floor to rescue her camper.

Dan stayed where he was, watching as Rebecca positioned herself protectively near the dark-haired girl. Adam didn't budge, though—and Dan gave the kid a silent cheer. Anyone, man or boy, who stood up to Rebecca Pruitt was just fine with him.

"Guys," Jimmy bellowed through the microphone, "you're not dancing."

"*You* dance, twinkle-toes!" one of the boys taunted Jimmy.

"All right, all right," Jimmy said, removing the Stones record and flipping it over. "We'll do a multiplication dance."

The campers responded with a chorus of groans.

Jimmy continued blithely, "Remember, ladies and gents, the only rule is, if someone asks you to dance you've *got* to say yes. Okay, folks, let's get started. Danny?"

Dan took a step farther into the barn. "Yeah?"

"Dan Macklin is going to start us off," Jimmy announced to the crowd. "Go ahead, Dan, pick a partner."

Dan's instinct was to pick Rebecca. But if he did, he'd get to dance with her only for a minute before Jimmy would stop the music and ask them to choose new partners.

He sought her with his gaze. She was watching him expectantly. He grinned at her, strode directly toward her...and snagged the hand of Stephanie Glynn. "I've got my partner," he called to Jimmy as he ushered the girl to the dance floor, aware that both Rebecca and Adam were gaping at him.

Stephanie was gaping at him, too, her head tilted back and her dark eyes wide and shimmering. "You're the Camp Mohawk director, aren't you?" she murmured in awe.

"You guessed."

She giggled faintly. "Do you know how to dance?"

"I most certainly do. Why wouldn't I?"

"I don't know," she said, giggling again. "You're so old."

He scowled good-naturedly. Jim started the music, a lively song. Dan began dancing with her, fifties style. She did her best to keep up, but her perpetual giggling interfered with her concentration, and she stumbled more than once in her laceless canvas sneakers.

In less than a minute Jimmy stopped the music. "Go pick a dance partner," Dan urged her, pointing her toward the boys' side of the room.

As soon as he released her hand, she turned and headed back to the girls' side, where Adam Kember awaited her. She chose him. He shot a swift, victorious look at Dan, who countered with a congratulatory smile.

Lifting his gaze, he saw Rebecca watching him again. She rested against a table, her arms crossed and her lips pursed. He headed toward her, and she straightened up and started to unfold her arms. But he strode right past her and offered his hand to a chubby girl with red hair and round cheeks. *"Mademoiselle,"* he said with a courtly bow.

Like Stephanie Glynn, the red-headed girl giggled.

The multiplication dance lasted at least ten minutes, by the end of which time Dan had danced with over a dozen gigglers—and spent each and every dance wishing his partner were Rebecca. Sometime during the dance he noticed that she had left her post by the table, and as he danced with a tall, gawky girl who made him think of Olive Oyl in orthodontic braces, he skimmed the increasingly crowded dance floor to see whom Rebecca was dancing with.

He couldn't find her. He saw three Chippewa counselors, one of them dancing with one of his counselors and looking quite pleased about it, but he couldn't locate Rebecca among the spinning, bouncing bodies.

An irrational anger seized him, followed by panic. Where had she gone off to? Her marital status notwithstanding, he had intended to dance with her at some point, when the floor was crowded and they wouldn't be so much in the spotlight. After bypassing her enough times to irritate her, he'd figured he would swoop down upon her and redeem her from her sulk. They would dance and she would gaze up into his eyes the way she had outside the barn.

Dan skimmed the room with his gaze, searching for a suitable Popeye for his Olive Oyl. He found a shy boy leaning against the wall, led the girl over, put them together and darted out of the barn.

He spotted Rebecca almost at once, strolling up the path that led around the administration building and down to the waterfront. Glimpsing Dan, she smiled and accelerated her stride. "Hi," she said.

He felt absurdly relieved to have found her. It wasn't as if she'd been lost or in danger, and it certainly wasn't as if sharing a dance with her was going to mean anything in the long run. Yet seeing her as she ambled along the path in those tantalizing little sandals, with the dusk light casting mysterious shadows across her face and her hair swinging loosely about her shoulders, filled him with delight.

Not that he'd ever let her know how thrilled he was to see her. He adopted a look of disapproval. "Don't tell me you're ready to abdicate responsibility so soon. We're supposed to be chaperoning this wingding, you know."

"I didn't mean to abdicate responsibility," she said, covering the last few yards in a lope. "I just—I was looking for one of my staffers."

"Oh?" He thought he'd seen all three Chippewa counselors inside the barn.

"She's a kitchen worker," Rebecca explained. "She'd never been to Mohawk before, and I told her she could ride over with us on the bus."

Dan remembered the older teenager who'd disembarked with the Chippies. "Where is she?" he asked.

"She's fine," Rebecca said. "She's making friends with one of your staffers."

"Oh." Making friends, was she? The way Dan wished he could make friends with Rebecca? "I was going to ask you to dance," he admitted, "but I didn't know where you were."

Her eyebrows rose slightly. "You could have asked me to dance at the beginning of that multiplication game."

His gaze locked with hers. It dawned on him that while he had revealed more than he should have, so had she.

"We could dance now," he said.

She eyed the barn, then glanced over her shoulder at the path she'd just taken. "Okay."

He took her hand. It was a natural gesture for a man who'd just asked a woman to dance, and she didn't balk at it. Instead, she wove her slender fingers through his and let him escort her back into the barn. He pretended that the smooth, cool feel of her hand within his didn't send a charge through his body, that the way her shoulder brushed his upper arm didn't fill his mind with all sorts of erotic ideas.

The dance floor was crowded enough that no one noticed they were holding hands. The song Jimmy played was a soulful, sexy ballad. Dan swept Rebecca into the midst of the dancing throng.

As if to counter the song's provocative lyrics, Rebecca maintained a discreet distance between her body and Dan's as he placed his hand at the small of her back. "The Pointer Sisters," she said, identifying the vocalists.

"Do you like them?"

"Yes. I'm not so sure the campers do, though."

He glanced around him. The younger couples on the dance floor were dancing mighty close, their arms ringed tightly around each other, their heads resting on each other's shoulders, their feet hardly moving. Dan suffered a pang of envy.

"I think the kids are enjoying the music well enough," he said, observing the couple closest to him. The girl had her face buried in the hollow of the guy's neck. Dan wished Rebecca would follow her lead.

Respecting the need to present a decorous example for the teenagers, however, he kept his right hand planted virtuously on her waist. Her head was up, her face far enough from his that he could see her clearly.

Looking at her wasn't bad, either, he consoled himself. It wasn't as good as having her body molded to his and her lips pressed into the warm skin beneath his jaw, but it wasn't bad.

"You don't have much in the way of current hits, do you?" she remarked.

"The camp hasn't got a CD player. Nowadays everything is formatted for CD."

"It's just as well," she said. "I like the older music better."

Even with her head back and her posture rigid, he was keenly aware of how she felt in his arms. He appreciated her physique, slim but not fragile. She had legs that could walk great distances, arms that could swim or paddle a canoe or hug a child, shoulders that could carry a backpack, hands that could lash branches into a shelter or wipe away a homesick camper's tears. She had the sort of body that prompted more than simple lust.

Complex lust, he decided with a sigh. "Tell me about your fiancé," he said, a self-protective move.

Her gaze narrowed on him. The electrical storm he had envisioned earlier swept through her silver-gray eyes now. They glinted with brilliant flashes of light, frightening yet magnificent. She opened her mouth and then shut it, apparently uncertain about what to say.

He wished she would move her lips again. They were so pink and soft and delicately shaped.

"I'd rather not talk about him," she finally said.

"Why not?"

"I'm here at Silver Lake. He's in New York. We're separated for the summer, and..." She exhaled. "I just don't want to talk about it."

"Oh." He wasn't sure what her cryptic statement meant, but he chose to interpret it as permission to pull her closer to him.

Before she could either sink against him or back off, the song ended. He kept his arm snugly around her, inhaling the fresh herbal fragrance of her hair, gauging the slender dimensions of her waist, wishing he could pull her just an inch closer for just a moment longer.

He didn't dare. "Thanks for the dance," he said, letting his hands drop.

Her lips parted again. He waited, thinking not about what she was about to say but about what she would do if he were insane enough to gather her to himself again and slide his tongue along the edge of her teeth. She would probably resolve, then and there, to tell him about her fiancé in gory detail—or else she'd bloody his nose.

Before she could say anything, Adam's counselor wove through the crowd to Dan and tapped his shoulder. "Excuse me, Dan?"

Pete's intrusion effectively broke the spell Rebecca had cast over Dan. He was grateful that Pete had brought him back to reality, but kind of sorry, too. "What's up?"

"We're running low on soda. Do you want me to go bring up another case from the mess hall?"

"No, that's all right. I'll get it."

"The mess hall—that's the dining room, right?" Rebecca spoke up, her eyes still flashing mysteriously.

"'Mess hall' is the manly term," he informed her with a smile. "We've got lots of soda stocked up in the refrigerator—we bring it up here one case at a time so it doesn't get warm."

"I can help you get it," she said.

"If you want to," he said. "But it's really no big deal. I can run down and back in five minutes."

"I'll keep you company."

He wondered why she was so eager to assist him in this trivial chore. It would be fun to believe that after one slow dance with him, she was so transported she couldn't bear to be parted from him even for a few minutes.

Fun but stupid. She wanted to help because she was one of the two presiding officers at the social. There was nothing more to it than that.

Shrugging nonchalantly, he took Rebecca's elbow and steered her through the swarm of campers to the door and outside. The sun had finished setting, bleeding the trees of color and leaving behind a sky of royal blue. Fireflies winked above the scraggly grass that grew alongside the path. The farther he and Rebecca walked from the barn, the more muted the sounds of music and chatter became, the more vivid the sounds of crickets and cicadas.

"Nice night, isn't it?" he said, inhaling the tangy pine-scented air.

"You know what I'd love?" she asked. "If you would give me that tour of Camp Mohawk now."

He smiled down at her. She really did seem awfully attentive to him. One dance, and she wanted to erase her fiancé from her memory bank and take a private evening stroll with Dan.

This could turn out to be very interesting.

"Let me deliver the drinks to the barn, and then I'll show you around."

"This refrigerator—it's in the kitchen, right?"

His confidence was jarred by a brief stab of bemusement. Why was she so hung up on Mohawk's dining facilities? "Of course it's in the kitchen. Where else would it be?"

"Over at Chippewa," she said brightly, "we have a back entrance, so you don't have to walk through the dining room to get to the kitchen."

"We have one, too."

"So, we'll just go in that way, get the soda and leave?"

He felt less confidence and more bemusement. "Do you make a detailed blueprint of everything you do?" he asked. "Or do you plan just the really complicated stuff, like getting a case of soda?"

She had the decency to look abashed. "I'm only curious, Dan," she said testily. "I'm comparing the two camps. I find it useful to know how they differ and how they're the same."

"Sure," he grunted. Anyone would want to know how Mohawk's kitchen door differed from Chippewa's. What could be more sensible?

They journeyed around the administration building and headed down the path toward the mess hall. Dan slowed when he saw two figures hiking up from the water's edge. As they got closer, he recognized the larger of the two as Ryan Gossens, the head of the kitchen staff at Mohawk.

"Oh, look, there's Lisa!" Rebecca said, sounding enormously relieved.

Lisa. The staffer Rebecca had gone looking for earlier. Evidently Lisa had met Ryan and they'd gotten friendly really fast. Even in the gloom Dan could see Ryan's toothy grin. Lisa looked pretty happy herself.

"Hi, Rebecca," Lisa said as the two couples neared each other on the path. The young woman turned her winsome smile to Dan. "You must be Dan Macklin."

"Dan, this is Lisa Rubin," Rebecca hastily introduced them. "We're going to the kitchen to get some more soda for the social."

Lisa's glowing smile faded. "You're going to the kitchen?"

"Say, Dan," Ryan interjected, "why don't Lisa and I bring the soda back up to the barn? I mean, it looks like you've got better things to do." His gaze traveled from Dan to Rebecca and back again.

From where Dan stood, it looked as if Ryan had better things to do, too. But before Dan could decline Ryan's offer of help, Lisa said, "Yeah, you two can get back to the dance, or whatever..."

Dan cast Rebecca a quick look. Her smile seemed genuine, but he couldn't shake the notion that something strange was going on—especially when she slipped her hand around his arm and asked him for that tour. Was this the same woman who'd wished him a watery death not long ago? Who'd warded him off by raising her fiancé up in front of her like a crucifix, as if to fend off a vampire attack? Who'd reacted to his silly little practical joke with icy anger?

All right, so she was thawing. A few days in the beautiful environs of Silver Lake, a pair of skimpy red sandals to set the tone, a few minutes in Dan's arms, dancing to that sensuous song about a man with a slow hand... and now she wanted a tour.

Maybe something strange was going on—or maybe he was just getting lucky.

"The tour," he said, smiling and tucking her hand more firmly against him, "is about to begin."

Chapter Four

Rebecca pulled off her sandals and lowered her feet into the water. Her toes scattered the moon's reflection on the lake's surface, but after a few seconds the water grew still once more and all the slivers of light regrouped into a new silver semicircle about her ankles.

The water was warm. So was the air. So was her mood.

She didn't want to like Dan Macklin. But during the course of his tour she'd found herself ... well, warming to him.

She had urged him to show her around Camp Mohawk only as a way of keeping him as far as possible from the dining room so he wouldn't discover the booby-trapped glasses. But as they strolled along the dirt paths that meandered through the camp, she found herself actually enjoying his company.

In the course of their walk, he stopped in at one bunkhouse where a counselor informed him that a camper was having nightmares about monsters in the woods. Dan excused himself and went inside to talk to the boy. Through the screened doorway Rebecca listened to his voice, soft and soothing and filled with gentle humor.

"Everybody has nightmares sometimes," Dan assured the boy. "The toughest kids in your bunk have them. Your counselors have them. Even I—the Head Hawk—have them. But then you wake up, shake it off and that's it. Okay?"

"Okay," the boy said.

"Now, get a good night's rest, pal, because tomorrow I'll be counting on you to help me clear the monsters out of my office."

Rebecca heard the boy laugh. A few seconds later Dan rejoined her, looking not the least bit smug about his success in vanquishing the child's fear.

The Camp Mohawk tour concluded at the swimming dock. It seemed a good place to stop—peaceful, secluded, offering a tranquil panorama of stars and moonlight and silhouetted trees and dark, placid water. Vertical pilings extended above the planks, providing convenient backrests when Rebecca and Dan lowered themselves to sit.

Maybe she shouldn't have pulled off her sandals and splashed her feet into the water. It wasn't the most decorous, professional thing to do. But she felt amazingly comfortable with him, comfortable enough to go barefoot.

What had begun as a ploy to keep him away from his mess hall had turned into something else. Trailing her bare toes through the water, Rebecca attempted to figure out exactly what that something was. Friendship? Genuine respect? Simple pleasure at finding herself alone with an unreasonably attractive man?

She tried to convince herself that she didn't have to like Dan just because he had a way with his campers. She didn't have to like him just because he was funny and sensitive.

She didn't have to like him just because his eyes, a dark green like the shadowy foliage arching above the lakeshore, caused her nerve endings to quiver with awareness.

"So, what do you think of my camp?" he asked.

"It's very nice," she said mildly. "Very different from Chippewa."

"Much more manly," he declared in an artificially gruff voice.

She caught his grin and mirrored it. "I'm not sure that's anything to brag about. I intend to run Camp Chippewa as a very womanly camp this summer."

"Womanly," he repeated, his tone now low and suggestive. "I like the sound of that."

She shook her head. "I didn't say 'ladylike' or 'girlish.' Do you know what womanly means?"

"Of course I do. It means looking sexier than an inflatable doll in black lace undies."

She refused to let his needling rile her. "It means being strong and unafraid."

"Ah." Dan's eyes glinted enigmatically. "And by that definition, are you womanly?"

"We're talking about my campers." She plowed ahead in an admirably even voice. "I've heard that in summers past, the Chippewa girls spent more time styling each other's hair than cooking over open fires.

Girlie stuff is fine in its place, but this is summer camp. The girls need to discover their strengths and develop them.''

"Do they, now."

"According to Maggie Tyrell, Chippewa has never once won the water Olympics against Mohawk."

"That's not a matter of developing their strength," Dan argued. "It's innate ability. The Hawks just happen to be superior when it comes to swimming and boating."

She sent him a confident smile. "We'll see about that."

Dan sent back an equally cocky one. "What other changes are you planning?"

"Well, there's the all-camp bus trips, for one. There's a summer stock theater not far from here—did you know that?"

He nodded. "Up near Monticello somewhere."

"They're staging *Peter Pan* this summer. I think that's something all the campers would enjoy."

Dan shook his head. "Going to the theater sounds suspiciously ladylike to me."

"I'm trying to broaden the girls' experience."

"You're trying to turn them into broads?"

She kicked water in his direction, but the flying droplets didn't come close to striking him.

He laughed. "Go ahead, broaden your Chippies. Make your mark. It's your show this summer. You may as well make the most of it."

"I intend to," she declared. "A few of the staff have told me that Chuck did this or that thing differently, but I want to do things my own way. I haven't received any complaints yet, so I may as well keep going."

"Change can be a positive thing," Dan remarked. "Chuck's been running Chippewa for close to ten years. Not that I'd wish a heart attack on him, but maybe the camp could use a director with a fresh outlook."

Rebecca was surprised by Dan's expression of support—and inordinately flattered. Obviously he was as adept at saying the right thing as he was at saying the wrong thing. He could encourage her as easily as he could skewer her.

"You're good at this, aren't you?" she said.

The moonlight glanced off his face, emphasizing its intriguing lines and angles. "Good at what?"

Keying into people's emotions. Affecting their moods for better or worse with a few well-chosen words. Soothing distressed little boys and reassuring novice camp directors. "Running Camp Mohawk," she said, refusing to let the conversation drift into personal territory.

"Yes," he said matter-of-factly. "I'm damned good at it."

She smiled at his lack of modesty. "Are you a good teacher?"

"One of the best."

"Awfully sure of yourself, too, aren't you?"

"I happen to be a terrific teacher," he countered with a shrug. "I'm not going to deny it."

"Do you teach in a public or a private school?"

"Public. I teach high school English in Pleasant Valley, over in Westchester County. It's a quiet suburban town. We don't have the sort of troubles city schools have, thank God." He folded his arms behind his head and regarded her with a canny grin. "Then again, I suppose that at the Piedmont School for prissy sissies—"

"The Claremont School," she corrected him. "And the students aren't prissy sissies. They're bright girls who want the kind of education you can't always get in a public city school."

"And who have tons of money to pay for it."

"A lot of them attend Claremont on scholarship," she said, refusing to acknowledge that the vast majority of Claremont's students came from privileged circumstances much like her own. She was a product of one of Manhattan's finest private schools herself.

"Do you do any teaching, or are you just a desk jockey?" he asked.

"I'm a dean, but I'm hardly a desk jockey." She traced a circle in the water with her big toe. "I fill in when someone on the faculty is sick, I direct special enrichment programs and one-on-one tutoring and I teach after-school programs in wilderness skills."

"Wilderness skills in New York City?"

"Why not? Just because Claremont students live in the city doesn't mean they can't get out and enjoy nature." She bit her lip to silence herself. She didn't have to justify herself or her school to Dan. Her position as a dean was as valid as Dan's position as a high school teacher.

Valid, perhaps, but...as an administrator, Rebecca knew better than most people how special teachers really were.

Dan would be a talented teacher; she hadn't needed him to tell her that. She'd observed him with his campers. He was good with children, no doubt about it.

"So," he said, regarding her from beneath slightly lowered lids, "are you going to keep working after you get married?"

Her first impulse was to chew him out for insinuating that being married might in any way interfere with her career. She checked that impulse, however. She *wasn't* about to get married. How could she scold him for jumping to conclusions about her impending marriage when she'd been untruthful about it a week ago, when she'd thought of Dan as a pain in the neck, undeserving of the truth?

She traced another arc through the water with her toe, studying the pattern of ripples it left in its wake. "You know, Dan..." She hesitated, questioning the wisdom of coming clean. Yes, she admired him. Yes, he had a way with youngsters. Yes, dancing with him had been fun.

Yes, he had the most heavenly eyes and the most devilish grin...and she could wind up in big trouble with him if she wasn't extremely cautious.

But caution didn't require dishonesty. Even though she was never going to be anything more than a colleague and a friend to Dan Macklin, she felt a compulsion to get rid of the lie hanging between them.

"I'm not really engaged," she confessed.

"Not formally."

"Not at all. I mean..." She sighed and forced herself to meet his gaze. He smiled benignly. "I *was* engaged until about a month ago. And it was very, very formal."

She watched the transformation in his face, from amusement to curiosity to comprehension to an almost wistful resignation. "In other words, you're recovering from a broken heart."

"No. I mean, not exactly." She sighed again. She should have kept her mouth closed. She'd made a mistake mentioning her engagement in the first place, and now she was compounding her mistake by raising the subject again.

The damage was done, though, and she saw no other option but to continue. "I was the one to end the engagement," she told him. "It was my choice. But... it was an intense thing, and I guess I still have some healing to do. I don't mean to be presumptuous, Dan, but you may as well know this about me. I've just gotten out of a heavy relationship. I'm not looking for a summer flirtation."

"I always thought flirting was the best way to get over a breakup," he said.

"You probably think flirting is the best way to get over anything."

"I probably do," he agreed, his smile widening until she could see his dimples plainly.

From the direction of the barn she heard the sounds of music and laughter. From the lakeshore to her left she heard the splash of an animal—a frog, perhaps—diving into the water. She felt terribly exposed to Dan, vulnerable to him. It made her uneasy.

"How formal is 'very, very formal'?" he asked.

She sized him up. As vulnerable as she felt, she sensed a certain kinship with him. He was here, after all, at Silver Lake, skirting the border of civilized life. He was here in the woods, surrounded by Mother Nature, appreciating that camping was as fulfilling as eating off china and that working with kids was as worthwhile as earning big bucks in a high-rise office.

No one back home understood why she'd broken up with Wallace. Not Wallace, who had offered her what he considered an irresistible package of matrimonial benefits. Not her friends, who had all thought he was a phenomenal catch. Certainly not her parents, who considered her the black sheep of the family and who had hoped that she would redeem herself by marrying a Wall Street attorney like Wallace and settling down to a properly affluent existence, one that had no room in it for sleeping beneath the stars.

No one in the city understood. But Dan wasn't like her family and friends. She could look at his scruffy hair and his callused hands and know that he would see things differently.

"It was so formal," she answered, "that the engagement party was held at the Plaza, with engraved invitations from Tiffany."

Dan's eyebrows arched high. "Wow. The air must be pretty thin up there."

"Breathe it long enough, and it can make you dizzy." She grinned. "That's why I jumped at the opportunity to leave Manhattan and take this job. My brain was desperate for oxygen."

"Did you have to return all the presents?"

"We didn't have presents. I requested that everyone make a donation to the Fresh Air Fund instead."

"And then you rushed off for some fresh air yourself."

Rebecca experienced a twinge of bittersweet loss as she remembered her year-long relationship with Wallace, her struggles to reconcile herself to him and to bend him a little toward her way of seeing things. "Maybe if Wallace had been willing to leave the city and come camping with me every now and then, I'd still be engaged to him. He has no interest in the great outdoors, though. He maintains that God gave us internal-combustion engines so we would never have to hike. And he hates camping. He claims he tried it once and it was too dirty."

"I've dated a few women who complained that everything I did was too dirty," Dan commented.

Rebecca chuckled in spite of herself. "I believe it."

Their quiet laughter caught on a breeze and drifted out onto the lake. She was once again aware of how isolated they were. The barn and the cabins of sleeping campers seemed far away. Her discord with her family back in New York—even her summer home on the opposite shore of Silver Lake—all seemed remote and insignificant. The only things that mattered were the lake itself and the moon.

And Dan.

Where was her common sense, her self-protectiveness? Where were her survival instincts? Why did his eyes look less green to her now than a dark blue glittering with inner light, a reflection of the starlit night sky? What strange urge made her want to lean toward him as he leaned toward her, made her yearn to brush her fingertips across his cheek, and slide her hand over his shoulder to his back, and touch her lips to his and taste the curve of his mischievous, marvelous smile?

Why did she feel so reckless all of a sudden, so willing to mess up her life?

She knew, as surely as she knew her own name, that if she leaned just a fraction of an inch closer to Dan, he would kiss her. And she knew that once he did, it would mess up her life to a disastrous degree.

Yet when she gazed into his eyes and saw him staring at her with such intensity, with such raw hunger, she couldn't seem to keep herself from desiring him. Her peripheral vision caught the movement of his hand reaching for her shoulder. Her breath lodged in her throat as he shifted closer, as his smile waned, as his gaze drew her in....

"Rebecca? Are you down there?"

She jerked back and spun around. One of her counselors was jogging down the path to the waterfront. "Yes, I'm here," she said in a rusty voice. Behind her she heard the thump of Dan's hand pounding the dock in frustration.

She raised her feet out of the water and slid them into her sandals, all the while refusing to look at him. She ought to be relieved that Bridget had come bounding down the path when she had. If not for this timely interruption, Rebecca would have been lost.

"It's after nine-thirty. Chuck always ended the socials by nine-thirty," said Bridget as she slowed to a halt at the edge of the dock. She flickered a smile in

Dan's direction, then turned back to Rebecca. "I guess you lost track of the time, huh."

"I guess I did," Rebecca said tightly, shooting a quick, accusing glance at Dan. Surely he should have known what time the social was supposed to end. He hadn't bothered to mention it, though—because he'd been about to pounce.

He shrugged with feigned innocence, then grinned and stood. As soon as she had her sandals buckled, he folded his hands around hers and helped her to her feet.

His grip was too strong, the surfaces of his palms too hard, his fingers too thick. The subtle potency of his hands as they tightened on hers sent a charge through her system, informing her of how very lost she would have been if Bridget hadn't come along when she had. Rebecca tried to conjure up a memory of her first couple of meetings with Dan, with his stupid doll and his stupider jokes, but all she could think of was that his hands felt good on her. Much too good.

She hadn't just warmed to him. She'd grown perilously overheated. It was definitely time to leave.

"We've got to do this again sometime," he said, his voice gravelly with innuendo.

"Talk, you mean?" she stressed, wriggling her hands free of his.

His eyes sought hers, eloquent with desire and a clear warning that he was as conscious as she was of how close they'd come to crossing a certain line. "Talk dirty."

"I thought you said our function at these socials was to set an example for the campers," she muttered, sounding unnecessarily contentious to herself. "We shouldn't have stayed away so long."

Ignoring her feisty tone, he slid his arm around her shoulders and escorted her up the dock to the shore. If Bridget hadn't been standing there, watching them, Rebecca would have elbowed Dan in the stomach. But in front of a witness, she felt obligated to maintain her poise, to pretend that Dan's casual hold on her was simply a gesture of camaraderie.

"We don't have to talk dirty," he promised. "We can just talk."

"Why do I have trouble believing you'd be satisfied with just talking?" she murmured under her breath.

The grin he tossed her was so frankly carnal she felt her cheeks burn. "Because I wouldn't be," he whispered, then slid his arm from around her as they joined up with Bridget on the path back to the barn. "For someone who claims to know wilderness skills," he commented, "you're much too tame."

"The best way to succeed in the wilderness is to avoid letting it overtake you."

"That's your opinion."

"That's my opinion," she declared firmly.

Hours later, as she lay awake on the cot in her cabin, once again allowing thoughts of Dan Macklin to interfere with her sleep, she questioned that opinion. Was it truly best to remain as tame as one could in the face of nature? Was it truly best to resist the wilderness?

Closing her eyes, she felt herself inundated by images of Dan, of his sparkling, variable eyes and his enticing smile and his strong hands. It was better to resist, she thought with a vague desperation. It was essential not to let the wilderness magic of her surroundings trick her into thinking a summer romance with Dan was worth risking.

Like Chuck DeVore, she had recently suffered a heart ailment—a spiritual one rather than a physical one, but just like Chuck she needed to recuperate. She needed to regain her bearings and clear the debris from her soul before she could even contemplate starting a relationship with another man.

Particularly a man like Dan. In his own clothed, clean-shaven way, he was the wilderness incarnate. He had a personality that was one part starlight and three parts gale-force wind, and a body that combined the speed of a cougar, the strength of a grizzly and the grace of a buck into something human and male and dangerously wild.

A manly man, she thought with a restless groan. Just what she didn't need.

OKAY, HE THOUGHT as he lay awake on the cot in his cabin, once again allowing thoughts of Rebecca Pruitt to interfere with his sleep. Okay, so she was convalescing from . . . from what? Not a broken heart, not a treacherous love affair, not a sordid, scandalous liaison, but rather a hoity-toity society engagement catered by the Plaza Hotel, with invitations from Tiffany.

What better course of treatment than to engage in a fun, no-strings-attached summer fling? What could be more appropriate than to spend some time doing dirty stuff with a high school teacher from Pleasant Valley, New York?

If only he'd had the chance to kiss her. For one breathless moment, with the crickets singing around them and the velvety night air closing in on them, the distance between Dan and Rebecca had seemed to compress like a spring, pulling them inexorably together. They'd come so close.

Just thinking about what might have happened if that Chippie counselor hadn't barged in on them was enough to condemn Dan to a chronic case of insomnia for the rest of the night—if not the rest of the summer.

Take what you can get, he advised himself. If a mutually satisfying translake fling wasn't in the cards, then at least he and Rebecca could be friends. At least they had gotten beyond the clenched-teeth verbal jousting that had marked their first few encounters. At least she'd thawed a bit toward him.

More than thawed. She had taken his arm and welcomed his company. She had danced with him not out of duty but because she'd wanted to. She had opened up and told him about herself.

She had told him she wasn't engaged, formally, informally or any other way. She was single, unattached, available—just like him.

His mind issued another warning that he shouldn't get his hopes up. But still, Rebecca had been so downright receptive to him, and when a hint of passion had crept into the air she'd felt it as strongly as he had. Her lips had parted, her eyes had widened, her breath had shortened and she'd moved toward him as he moved toward her, ready, willing and just as eager as he was.

Merely thinking about that moment, about the promise that had stretched taut and shimmering between them, caused his blood pressure and certain parts of his anatomy to rise. Why not let his hopes rise, too?

Eventually he drifted off to sleep. In his dream he was on the dock with Rebecca again, her pale hair turning to silver in the moonlight and blowing in delicate tufts back from her smooth, round cheeks. In his dream no one interrupted him as he neared her, as he slid his hand to the back of her head and pulled her against him. Her lips reminded him of a ripe peach, soft and sweet and bursting with the flavor of summer....

"Hey, Dan, wake up!"

"Huh?" He snorted, snuffled and squinted at his alarm clock. Eight o'clock. The alarm was supposed to rouse him at seven—but as soon as his eyes adjusted to the offensive brightness of the sun filtering through his shades, he noticed that he'd neglected to set it.

"Yeah," he growled in the direction of his cabin's door. "Yeah, I'm up."

"There's something you've got to see," Jimmy Angelini shouted through the closed door. "Come on, man—this is incredible!"

"Incredible," Dan muttered under his breath as he rubbed the last traces of sleep out of his eyes with his knuckles. He threw back the sheets, yanked on some clothes and shuffled to the door, bracing himself to

withstand his first confrontation with the dazzling morning sun.

Dan glowered at his wide-awake boating instructor. "What incredible thing do I have to see?" he muttered.

"It's down in the mess hall," Jimmy answered. "*Mess* hall," he reiterated, snickering to himself. "Saturday breakfast is at eight o'clock, Danny. You should have been up by now."

Dan checked the retort that sprang to his lips. Why snap at Jimmy? The sky was cloudless, the air warm and heavily scented with pine, the lake glinting a brilliant blue through the trees. Healthy young voices emanated from the mess hall in a cacophony of hooting and guffawing. His Hawks were happy. All was right with the world.

All would have been perfect with the world if he'd only gotten to kiss Rebecca last night.

As his eyes adjusted to the light and his brain shook off the last shadows of sleep, he raked his fingers through his uncombed hair. "What's going on in the mess hall?" he asked.

"You'll have to see for yourself." Jimmy nudged Dan ahead of himself down the path. They swung through the double doors into the mess hall—and Dan saw for himself.

Water. Water on the floor, water sloshing across the wooden picnic-style tables, flooding over the edges and spilling onto the attached wooden benches. Water dripping from the walls. Water puddling at Dan's feet.

Water trapped inside an overturned glass that stood on the table nearest the door.

"What the hell . . . ?"

"There were at least ten glasses like that on every table," Jimmy explained as an already soaked camper reached for the glass and lifted it with a popping, sucking sound. Water splattered in all directions. A few drops struck Dan's face.

He cursed. "Who did it?" he asked Jimmy. "One of our bunks?"

"Uh-uh. I think it happened last night. We had visitors, you know."

Chippies.

Dan cursed again. Chippies must have stolen into the mess hall while he was somewhere else.

With Rebecca.

His curse this time was aimed not at the flood conditions in the mess hall but directly at her. The two-faced witch! Favoring him with her beguiling smiles, imploring him to give her a camp tour, hinting with body language that she would welcome a kiss . . . and all she'd wanted was to keep him away from the mess hall while her accomplices sabotaged the joint.

Memories rushed at him: her bizarre questions about the kitchen door, her edginess when they'd gone down to get more soda, her relief when Ryan Gossens and her own junior counselor offered to get the sofa.

"Ryan," he groaned. "Where the hell is Ryan Gossens?"

"In the kitchen, I guess," Jimmy said.

"I'm going to kill him!" Dan sprinted through the room, ignoring the water that soaked through the seams of his shoes and splashed up onto his bare ankles, ignoring the hilarity of a hundred and eighty wet, obstreperous boys running amok in the mess hall.

Summer traditions and high jinks suddenly were forgotten. Rebecca Pruitt had led him on. She'd deliberately played up to him, all for this. If Ryan had abetted her in any way, the guy was dead meat.

"Gossens!" Dan bellowed as he stormed into the kitchen. Several kitchen staffers were lugging mops and buckets out from the storeroom; others were scurrying around, flipping pancakes and stacking them on serving platters.

Ryan Gossens stood in their midst, a full-length white apron tied around his waist and a white tennis hat set rakishly on his head. He set down his spatula and grinned at Dan. "Yeah, boss?"

"You were in on this, weren't you?"

Ryan's eyes grew round. "Who, me?"

Dan stalked through the kitchen to Ryan and grabbed his shirt in his fists. "Gossens, I'm warning you, if you helped those damned Chippies to pull this stunt—"

"Hey, man, chill out," Ryan chided him. "That's all it is, a stunt. It's summertime, Dan. Lighten up."

Dan took a deep breath, then relaxed his hold on Ryan. It *was* summertime. A time for fun and games. He was overreacting only because he'd believed that there had been something real going on between him and Rebecca last night, something she had felt as powerfully as he had.

So it was all a joke. So he was the one with the faulty sense of humor. He ought to be pleased that

Rebecca was willing to pick up where Chuck had left off.

After all, Dan had fired the first salvo in this war when he'd invaded her camp with his inflatable doll.

Now she'd gotten him.

Which meant, he acknowledged with a slowly dawning smile, that it was his turn to get her again.

Chapter Five

There were midnight specials, AK-47s, Colt six-shooters, carbines, futuristic zap guns and one remarkable contraption that operated on the same principle as a medical syringe, except that it was four feet long and promised to load a half-gallon of ammo at a time and shoot with reasonable accuracy.

Only a few stores in Monticello carried these water pistols. But Dan visited them all on Saturday afternoon and bought out their entire stock.

Rebecca Pruitt and her Chippies had declared war. Surrender was out of the question for Dan and his Hawks. And no matter how strong Rebecca intended to make her campers, pantywaist glasses of water were going to prove no match for the juicy firepower of Mohawk's manly men.

He had come a long way since his literally rude awakening that morning. Whatever might or might not develop between him and Rebecca, he was glad she had stopped behaving like the prep-school prig he'd originally taken her to be and had decided to get into the spirit of Silver Lake fun. Really, how far a leap was it from skirmishing to sex?

He plucked his sunglasses from the neckline of his T-shirt, where he'd hooked them while he'd been in the five-and-dime, and slid them up onto his nose. He had no pressing business back at camp—the Hawks were probably washing up for dinner right now, after which the camp would sponsor its weekly "Saturday Night at the Movies." Tonight's feature was the second *Star Trek* flick. Dan had seen it a dozen times already, and he wasn't needed back at camp.

On the other hand, the small Catskill village of Monticello didn't exactly offer a dazzling choice of weekend entertainment. He supposed he could grab a couple of slices of pizza, maybe catch a ball game on the wide-screen TV in one of the bars....

Damn, but he missed Chuck. If Chuck were available, they'd be drinking together. Doing it alone would only make Dan lonely for his buddy.

Sighing, he dug his keys out of the front pocket of his jeans. Before he could unlock his car door, he spotted a familiar-looking woman across the street. She had her back to him, and her floral-print sundress momentarily misled him. But he recognized the shiny corn-colored hair falling down past her shoulders, and her shoulders themselves, graceful without being overly dainty. He recognized the neat proportions of her figure, flaunted by the cinched waist of her dress, and her lovely legs, bare and a tawny golden color, and most of all her ridiculously tiny feet in their saucy red sandals.

She was with a man.

The erstwhile fiancé? Dan wondered, sizing up her companion. He, too, had his back to Dan; he stood beside Rebecca, reading the menu posted in the window of a coffee shop. He was dressed conservatively, in tailored slacks and a starchy white shirt, his gray-streaked dark blond hair trimmed with rigorous precision.

He must have come to the Catskills to woo Rebecca back. If Dan were a true friend, he would leave them alone to work out their problems.

But who said Dan was a true friend?

Grinning, he strolled across the street. "Hey, Becky!" he shouted with unwarranted familiarity. "If you're here and I'm here, who's minding the kids?"

Rebecca and her escort spun around. The man appeared to be too old for her. The hair at his temples was a solid gray, and it was thinning on top. The skin around his eyes and lips was creased, and his cheeks and chin appeared weathered from too many years of shaving.

Rebecca's eyebrows climbed her forehead, and her mouth slipped into a smile of surprise. "Dan! What are you doing here?"

"I had to pick up a few things," he answered, turning to her fiancé and giving him a closer inspection. Definitely too old. He looked like a well-preserved sixty-year-old. Very clean, though. Dan could understand how such an impeccably dapper man would find camping too dirty for his taste. "You have company, I see," Dan said, turning back to Rebecca expectantly.

"My father," she informed him. "Dad, this is Daniel Macklin, the director of Camp Mohawk, across the lake from Camp Chippewa. Dan, my father, Harrison Pruitt."

If he'd thought about it, Dan would have been unnerved by the depth of his relief at the news that the man was Rebecca's father. Why should he care if her former lover came to the Catskills to win her back?

Yet he *was* relieved. "How do you do, Mr. Pruitt," he said, extending his hand.

"Daniel, is it?" Her father's clasp was hard and domineering, contrasting with his reserved smile. "What a pleasure."

"My father came up to see Camp Chippewa," Rebecca said. "I thought I'd spare him the camp food and take him out for a real dinner."

"If you're looking for a good meal, there's a place around the corner that's better than this," Dan told them, gesturing toward a side street.

"I should hope it's better," Harrison Pruitt commented with a barely audible sniff. "This menu is rather limited, to say the least."

Rah-thah limited, Dan repeated to himself. Now he knew who the prig of the Pruitt clan was. "You didn't mention last night that your dad was coming to visit," he remarked to Rebecca.

Harrison blanched; the facial muscles holding his smile in place twitched. His glacial silver eyes flickered from Rebecca to Dan and back again. "You two were together last night?" he asked.

Swallowing a chuckle, Dan opened his mouth to correct her father's erroneous assumption. But before he could speak, Rebecca replied, "Yes, as a matter of fact, we were." She shot Dan an unreadable look and said, "Dad decided to come up at the spur of the moment. He called me at ten o'clock this morning to let me know his plans, and he arrived at the camp around two." Her eyes continued to send their inscrutable message to Dan. He shrugged slightly, and she gave him an almost imperceptible nod.

"You were together last night?" Harrison repeated, his tone even chillier than before.

Again, before Dan could speak, Rebecca said, "Yes." She gave Dan a sugary smile. "Why don't you join us for dinner, Dan? Now, where was that good restaurant you mentioned? Around the corner?"

She was up to something. This time, however, her father was the target of her duplicity. Dan knew that, whatever he'd just stumbled into, it wasn't going to leave him with wet shoes and a craving for revenge.

Not only was she up to something, but she needed Dan to make it work. He liked the idea of her needing him. He *loved* the idea of having her indebted to him. The whole situation was irresistibly interesting.

"Sure, I'll join you for dinner," he said, looping his arm around Rebecca's warm, bare shoulders and giving her a friendly squeeze. Refusing to release her even when he felt her discreet withdrawal, he started toward the corner, beckoning her father to keep up with them. "Come on, Mr. Pruitt, you're going to love this place. Follow me!"

THE THOUGHT OF following Dan Macklin anywhere left Rebecca with dire misgivings. She'd been a fool to invite him to dinner and even more of a fool to leave her father with the impression that there was anything more than friendship—and a dubious friendship, at that—between her and Dan.

Well, maybe there *was* something more between them. Whenever she let her attention stray, it zoomed back to last night at the waterfront, when Dan's lips had been a breath from hers and her soul had reached out for him, wanting him. What was between them was hot, alive and very dangerous. If she'd stopped to think, she would never have asked Dan to stick around for dinner with her father.

But she hadn't stopped to think. Anger tended to make her rash, and she was furious with her father.

He had scarcely emerged from his car when he'd begun what amounted to a nonstop tirade about what an appalling place Camp Chippewa was. *"This parking lot isn't paved,"* he'd groused as he and Rebecca had tramped across the gravel expanse. And, *"Your office isn't even air-conditioned!"* and *"You actually live in this—this hovel?"*

For all his insistence that he'd driven to Camp Chippewa to see the place, the real reason for her father's abrupt visit was obvious: he wanted her to patch things up with Wallace. "He was over to dinner the other night," her father had informed her in a deceptively nonchalant voice. "The poor man is beside himself, you know."

Rebecca had been tempted to ask why her family was entertaining a man who was no longer a part of their lives, but to do so would only prolong the discussion, so instead she'd said, "Would you like to see the volleyball and archery areas?"

He'd refused to take the hint. "He's willing to forgive you, thank heavens. It's clear that he thinks you'll make a fine wife, once you get this juvenile summer-camp nonsense out of your system."

"It's not juvenile, it's not nonsense and I wouldn't make a fine wife for him."

"Rebecca, darling... Wallace is offering you the opportunity of a lifetime, to be the wife of a man destined for glory on Wall Street, to be the sort of woman society looks up to—"

"Society with a capital *S?*" Rebecca had muttered. "There'll be other opportunities, Dad."

"You're nearly thirty," he'd remarked ominously. "Wait much longer, and those opportunities will dry up." He'd ducked, then batted with his hands at the air beside his ear. "Good God! What's attacking me?"

Rebecca had spotted a pale green inchworm slithering down a silken strand from a tree branch above her father's head. "It's nature, Dad," she'd said with a wry smile. Taking her father's arm, she'd led him down the path to the waterfront. "Come on, I'll show you the boating dock."

Her father had given the canoes and rowboats a swift, condescending glance. "You call these boats? If you'd stayed home and resolved your problems with Wallace, you could have been spending weekends on his sloop in the Hamptons."

On and on, hour after hour, all afternoon long. *"If only you met him halfway.... If only you weren't so stubborn.... He quite adores you, Rebecca.... You're throwing away a life of comfort.... You aren't getting any younger...."*

Finally she'd given up on the possibility of getting any work done. She'd showered, changed into a dress and driven him to Monticello for dinner. At one of the few diners that promised something other than pizza, they had paused to peruse the menu. As she read the listings, Rebecca had tried to figure out a way to get her father to leave for the city immediately after dinner.

Then she'd heard Dan's voice calling to her, and a strange notion had flashed through her head: *salvation.*

An exceedingly strange notion. Of all the men in the universe, Daniel Macklin was arguably the one least likely to save her. Particularly after what Lisa Rubin had done to his mess hall last night at Rebecca's behest.

But still—what was the harm in letting her father think she and Dan were romantically involved? It might force him to acknowledge that Wallace was irretrievably in her past. It might force her father to accept that Rebecca had a life of her own, separated from her parents not simply by miles but by opinion and taste.

The moment Dan wrapped his arm around her shoulders, though, she realized that whatever he was offering her, salvation wasn't it. He was much too enthusiastic about her little scam, and his embrace was

entirely too possessive. When he gave her an affectionate squeeze before releasing her to open the door
of the restaurant around the corner, she was sorely
tempted to elbow him in the ribs.

What was that insight she'd had last night, about
how letting herself have anything to do with Daniel
Macklin was going to mess up her life? Already things
seemed to be unbearably messy.

Her father's gaze skittered from the linoleum floor
to the neon beer signs on the wall behind the counter,
from the vinyl-and-Formica decor to the gum-chewing
waitress who led them to a booth at the rear and
slammed three laminated menus onto the table. "This
is the *better* place?" Harrison muttered, his nostrils
pinched in disapproval.

"Don't judge a book by its cover," Dan said. "The
food's great."

Given her father's presumption that she and Dan
were a couple, Rebecca felt obliged to sit beside Dan
on the narrow banquette, across the table from her
father. Dan chivalrously gestured for her to slide in
first, and once he took his seat beside her she felt
trapped. He wasn't exactly crowding her, but... Even
with several inches of space between them, she was
uncomfortably conscious of his nearness, afraid of
shifting her leg the slightest bit and accidentally
bumping his thigh with hers, or his elbow, or any other
part of him.

She edged as close to the wall as she could without
being obvious about it and hid behind her menu.

"I don't suppose they have a wine list," Rebecca's
father grumbled.

Dan laughed, as if her father had been joking. Rebecca knew better; her father deemed unworthy of his patronage any restaurant lacking a proper selection of wines.

"The pastrami here is excellent," Dan told him.

"I'm sure it is," he said faintly. His nostrils narrowed once more as he perused the listings.

"They've got great pickles, too. That's what I'm going to order—a pastrami on rye, pickles on the side. How about you, honey?" he asked, slinging his arm around Rebecca's shoulders again.

She kicked him under the table, harder than she'd intended to. He grimaced and mouthed "Ow!" before removing his arm and turning back to her father.

"Did I tell you about the charming new bistro your mother and I went to?" her father said as he lowered his menu. "We were scouting the galleries on Madison Avenue and just happened to come across it. Lovely place. Fresh flowers everywhere, and the food was *très magnifique.*"

Rebecca could feel Dan's posture changing beside her. He squared his shoulders and zeroed in on her father with his gaze. For a brief moment she felt sorry for her father, and then she decided that after all his supercilious criticism that afternoon, he deserved whatever Dan gave him.

"Do you speak French, Mr. Pruitt?" he asked. "The ultimate romance language, I call it. *Langue de l'amour.* The tongue of love." With that, he launched into a long, mellifluous monologue in French.

Rebecca was fluent in Spanish and could understand dribs and drabs of German, but she'd never

learned French. Nevertheless, she was mesmerized by
the sparkle in his blue-green eyes, the sly dimple at the
corner of his mouth and the emphatic motions of his
hands. She glanced at her father, who appeared ap-
propriately sheepish about his ignorance of French,
and then turned back to Dan, whose smile had expanded slightly as he enjoyed his triumph over her father.

The tongue of love, she thought, suppressing a small
shudder deep within her.

Dan's speech was brought to a halt by the arrival of
their waitress, still popping what appeared to be a
three-stick wad of gum. "You folks ready to order?"
she asked.

"But of course," Dan said with just enough affec-
tation to remind Rebecca that, his mastery of French
notwithstanding, he was a scoundrel, far too eager to
lampoon her father. "What would please your pal-
ate, *ma cherie?*" he asked Rebecca.

She leaned around him to order for herself. "The
chicken-salad platter," she requested, "and an iced
tea."

Her father ordered a club steak, curling his lip as he
did so. Dan asked for the pastrami and a cola. "I
wonder what kind of wine would go with pastrami,"
he mused once the waitress had cleared away their
menus and departed.

"The kind that's drunk directly from the bottle,"
Rebecca muttered.

"It sure is nice to eat out every now and then," Dan
continued blithely. "It's especially nice to eat in a *dry*
place, with *dry* floors." He paused long enough to let

that sink in, then said to her father, "We have a real mildew problem. Not so much in the mess hall as in the bunks. The kids leave their wet towels on the floor, all bunched up, until the stink is practically toxic. Southeasterly winds, and you could probably smell it even in Manhattan."

"What an appetizing thought," Rebecca's father grumbled.

"One summer, a couple of years back, we had so much rain one week that fungus started growing on the floorboards. Tiny beige mushrooms. It was amazing."

"I'm sure."

"But that's what roughing it's all about," Dan went on. "Mold and mildew, overturned glasses and water on the dining-room floor... all part and parcel of the Silver Lake experience." She was about to shut him up when he turned to her and asked, "Have your campers had any food fights yet?"

"No." She couldn't bluntly tell him to stifle himself, because she wanted her father to think she and Dan had a relationship. If she could convince her father that rude men were more to her taste than paragons of etiquette, maybe her father would stop trying to persuade her to reconcile with Wallace.

"My junior boys really went at it the other day," Dan related, generously including Rebecca's father in the conversation. "We were having spaghetti—or pasta, as you might call it. Actually the campers called it 'slime tinsel.' They had a contest to see who could loop the most strands of spaghetti over the rafters in the mess hall."

"Perhaps, as their leader, you might consider setting a more civilized tone," her father commented.

"Civilization has its place," Dan agreed, oozing polite respect. "Its place just doesn't happen to be Silver Lake. Summer camp is a time for getting down and dirty. Isn't that right, Becky?"

She was tempted to castigate him for using that girlish nickname without her permission. Wallace had never called her Becky; she could no longer recall when they'd discussed it, but she distinctly remembered him once snapping, "I have no intention of becoming Tom Sawyer to your Becky."

All right, then—Dan *could* call her Becky, if only to make him even less Wallace-like.

"A little dirt can't be avoided," she conceded. "But I *never* get down."

"We'll see about that." Dan's smile brimmed with challenge.

"Actually I happen to agree with my father that it's the director's job to set the proper tone at the camp."

"Sure," Dan concurred, his smile growing deliciously mischievous. "The tone at Camp Mohawk is fun. What's the tone at Camp Chippewa?"

"You don't have to wallow in the dirt to have fun."

"No, but you can't have fun if you're worrying about staying clean all the time. Particularly at camp. Now take today," he said, once again widening his focus to include Rebecca's father. "We had a worm contest at Mohawk."

She nudged Dan's ankle with her toe. A little joking was one thing, but a conversation about worms at the dinner table went too far.

He responded to her under-the-table warning with a determined smile. "It's for fishing. Do you do any fishing, Mr. Pruitt?"

The subject seemed to perk Rebecca's father up. "I've done some sport fishing down in the Caribbean," he said. "Marlin, barracuda... Needless to say, we didn't use worms for bait."

"Still," Dan countered, "there's nothing quite as thrilling as a successful worming expedition. Bunk Four won this week's contest. Bunk Three would have won, but they cheated. When we dumped their worms out onto the barn floor, we discovered they'd padded their bucket by mixing in a few handfuls of snails. That's what you would call *escargot*," he added for Rebecca's father's benefit.

Her father pursed his lips and surveyed the dining room. "If you'll excuse me, I believe I'll use the facilities." He stood, sent Rebecca a scathing look and stalked across the restaurant, refusing to acknowledge the waitress, who passed him carrying a tray with their food to the table.

Rebecca watched her father's departure with a mixture of amusement and dismay. He had given her a hard time all afternoon, yet she felt sorry for him. She knew from nerve-racking personal experience what it was like to be tormented by Dan Macklin.

Dan was behaving abominably. And the juvenile grin he gave her once the waitress was gone made her want to kick him again, not in his ankle or shin but higher up, somewhere that would leave him squeaking for the next few months.

"What's wrong with you?" she ground out.

His smile didn't waver. "I give up. What's wrong with me?"

"How can you act so gross?"

"Gross? I thought I was being scintillating. More scintillating than your father."

"Leave my father out of this—"

"You brought him into this, Becky, old girl."

"He brought himself into it," she admitted reluctantly. It was true; he should have stayed back in the city commiserating with poor, brokenhearted Wallace. "I would appreciate it if you didn't discuss worms and food fights anymore for a while."

"What's the matter? Too dirty for you?"

"Yes." She lifted her fork and surveyed her plate. A hemisphere of chicken salad sat atop a limp leaf of lettuce. She poked the stiff celery-dotted mound with the tines of her fork.

"Why did you include me in this dinner?" Dan asked, all traces of mocking gone from his voice.

"Because my father's an arrogant twit," she admitted with a dismal sigh. "I figured . . ." She drifted off, unsure of how to continue.

"You figured you'd blow the guy away by letting him think we were intimate?"

Merely hearing Dan use the word "intimate" rattled her. "I don't want him interfering with my social life," she said.

"Am I part of your social life?" Dan asked with far too much interest.

"Don't flatter yourself." She poked at the salad again. "What was all that stuff you were saying in French?"

"Does your father understand French?"

"No."

"Thank God." He flashed her a smile, then took a bite of his sandwich. "It's an old joke about a fisherman, a mermaid and a sea cucumber. Would you like me to translate it for you?"

"Spare me. And please, spare my father, too."

"Do you really want me to spare him?"

She searched his eyes. They glowed with warm humor, not cool mockery. No matter what was going on between her and Dan, Rebecca recognized that if she asked him to spare her father right now, he would.

"It's just . . ." She sighed and turned away, disconcerted by Dan's sudden earnestness. "My father is not a fan of the great outdoors."

"Then why is he visiting?"

"He's trying to persuade me to work things out with Wallace."

"Your fiancé."

"My *ex*-fiancé." She prodded the salad with her fork once more, this time rupturing its surface. Having achieved that small victory, she reached for her iced tea and took a long sip.

"If you don't want to work things out with Wallace," Dan advised her, "why don't you just tell your father point-blank? Tell him you don't want to spend the rest of your life with an arrogant twit and leave it at that."

"Wallace isn't an arrogant twit," she argued. "He's a nice man."

"Oh. A *nice* man." The way Dan said it, "nice" sounded like the ultimate insult. "Well, if he's all that nice, marry him."

"Don't simplify my life, all right?" she snapped, realizing as soon as she'd spoken that more than anything else, simplifying her life was what she needed to do.

Her father's words echoed inside her. She was nearly thirty. Opportunities were going to dry up. He hadn't quite come out and said *she* was going to dry up, but his implication was clear.

She loved working with the girls of Camp Chippewa, just as she'd loved teaching adolescents Outward Bound skills, just as she'd loved teaching fifth-grade kids down in North Carolina and overseeing the students at Claremont. She yearned for a child of her own. If she married Wallace, she could have all the children she wanted.

But he would balk if she ever tried to take them camping. "They'll get dirty," he would object.

An oppressive sadness fell over her. She stared blankly at her salad platter, stricken by the fact that what she wanted—a man mature enough to make a commitment to her but not so mature he was a bore—seemed beyond her reach.

Why did she insist on perfection, anyway? Maybe wanting more than what Wallace could offer was unreasonable.

Particularly since whenever she thought of what she wanted, she thought of Dan Macklin.

Definitely unreasonable. How could she possibly want someone so immature he took pleasure in nauseating her father with dinner-table conversation about worms and mildew?

How could she want someone so unstable his eyes didn't even stay one color, someone who thought life was one big laugh, someone who seemed at home and at peace beside a mountain lake, beneath a starry sky, who understood that clean sheets and air-conditioning weren't the most important things in the universe, who flourished in the clean pine-scented air above Silver Lake, whose strong arms could propel a canoe and comfort a child and arouse dark, trembling sensations inside Rebecca?

Wallace offered her marriage and security.

All Dan seemed to offer was trouble—and fun.

The hell with them both, she thought, plunging her fork savagely into the lump of chicken salad before her. The hell with men. She had three months to go before her thirtieth birthday, three months during which she would steer clear of the male species.

Once those three months were up . . . then she could start worrying about how to live the rest of her life.

Chapter Six

When her father departed from Silver Lake, he left behind rain clouds. Three days' worth. The first day it drizzled intermittently; the next two days it poured incessantly. By the time the sun returned on Wednesday, the arts-and-crafts counselor reported that she had overseen the creation of more than one hundred lanyards and at least fifty-seven ceramic ashtrays, and she demanded to be put out of her misery.

Rebecca gave her the morning off and organized the campers in a celebratory day of outdoor activities—softball and volleyball games, extra swim sessions, canoe races and, after supper and cleanup, a campfire on the beach. As the gloriously cloudless sky above the lake faded from blue to lavender to mauve, Rebecca and her staff doled out marshmallows for roasting and led the campers in a hootenanny.

Maybe her father was right in claiming that running a summer camp counted for little among polite society. To her, though, gathering around a campfire on the beach with a group of happy, high-spirited girls, singing and chanting and pigging out on charred marshmallows beneath a clear mountain sky, was the most worthwhile thing in the world. Rebecca felt a sense of communion and accomplishment, a recognition that she could run a camp well and bring joy to so many children—and she could do it without clean sheets and an air-conditioned office. She could survive rain and mud. She could get dirty and not consider herself a failure.

It wasn't until the loud singing ended that Rebecca heard the muted splashing noise behind her. Spinning around, she saw the boats. Dozens of them, possibly every boat in the Camp Mohawk fleet, each of them carrying several campers. The girls noticed, too. They ran to the water's edge and hurried out onto the swimming dock to greet the visitors from across the lake.

Realizing they'd been spotted, the boys began to snicker and hoot. They rowed closer, paddling in a ragtag formation. As her eyes adjusted to the twilight, Rebecca noted that they were wearing swimsuits. And then, as they moved even closer, she saw that they were armed.

"Look out!" she warned a second before the first volley struck. Water pistols squirted and spurted, dousing the Chippewa girls who had congregated on the dock.

Shrieks pierced the air. The girls, all showered and neat in their clean white Chippewa shirts, retreated from the assault. That only encouraged the boys to come closer to the shore, steering around the dock and bombarding the girls on the beach with their water ammunition.

Some of the girls fled from the waterfront area. Others—mostly the younger ones—returned fire, wading into the water and splashing handfuls of it up at the boats. A few enterprising Chippies charged toward the dining room in search of bowls and pitchers.

"Get out of the water, girls! Come on, get out!" a counselor shouted, trying to drag the waders back onto the beach. Not that it mattered; the girls were already drenched.

Rebecca thought grimly about how long it had taken the camp to dry out from three days of precipitation. Now, as she steered several campers behind some shrubs and watched the boys assail the magnificent bonfire with glistening arcs of water, she wondered how long it would take to dry everyone out again.

In the daytime, at the peak of the afternoon heat, when the campers had all been dressed for swimming, this might have been a funny stunt. But now, after days of soggy weather and short tempers, the whole camp had gathered for a beautiful evening of song and sisterhood. That the Mohawks would break up such a special moment infuriated her.

Granted, the campers were merely privates in this battle, only following orders. Their general was the one who deserved her wrath.

She stormed to the water's edge and surveyed the boisterous armada in search of its leader. With deft precision Dan Macklin wove through the horde in a sleek aluminum canoe. His hair was held off his face with a bandanna; his smile was repulsively cocky.

"Call them off!" she shouted as his canoe drew close. "It's enough, Dan! You've ruined our campfire. Now go away!"

His grin remained as he balanced his paddle across the sides of the boat and reached down. He lifted a huge tubelike contraption, dipped its tip into the water and loaded it.

Rebecca gaped at him, horrified. "Don't even think about it," she warned. "I'm already mad enough—"

Her final word was drowned out—literally—as a tide of cool lake water washed over her. Sputtering and gasping, she leapt back and shoved her heavy wet hair back from her face. "Dan, I mean it, I—"

Another gush hit her, square in the solar plexus. She reeled around, cursing when she heard the squishy sound of her drenched shoes.

"Dan, you have no right—"

A third volley, this one aimed at her breasts. Her shirt clung to her body, becoming vaguely translucent. Glancing down, she noticed the distinct puckering of her nipples against the wet fabric. She hastily yanked the shirt away from her skin and glowered at Dan.

"I'll get you back for this!" she roared.

He returned his loathsome weapon to the bottom of the canoe and nodded courteously. "I'm looking forward to it," he said, then grabbed his paddle, steered the prow back toward the eastern shore of the lake and hollered, "Okay, guys, head for home!"

Out on the lake the boys complained laughingly about how they were just warming up, how they'd wanted to stage a land assault like the Marines at Iwo

Jima. Behind her, Rebecca heard grumbling among her campers.

"Those guys are such weenies," one girl muttered.

"I swear, those creeps would follow Danny Macklin anywhere. . . ."

"So would I," another girl said dreamily.

"Yeah," someone sighed.

"You know," Maggie Tyrell remarked as she sidled up next to Rebecca, "Chuck DeVore would laugh it off."

Chuck DeVore wouldn't care if Dan Macklin saw him in a wet T-shirt, Rebecca retorted silently. "Just because we flooded his mess hall doesn't mean he had to do this," she muttered, once again peeling her limp shirt away from her skin.

"Sure it does," Maggie argued. Rebecca turned to her assistant, whose curly hair glistened with droplets of water and whose face and clothes were spattered. "And now you'll have to do something to him."

"I certainly will."

"Something really crude."

Rebecca permitted herself a small grin. "Macklin's the crude one. I doubt I can come up with anything to compare with this."

Lifting a sodden lock of hair from Rebecca's face and watching as water streamed down from it, Maggie chuckled. "You're much too mature and sophisticated, huh."

Rebecca's smile expanded into a faint laugh. "If lusting for revenge isn't mature, I guess I'm not all that mature."

"Glad to hear it," said Maggie, giving Rebecca's shoulder a reassuring pat before they turned and headed back to the waterlogged camp fire.

LONG AFTER HE'D GOTTEN his Hawks settled down, long after lights-out had quieted the camp and the counselors who weren't on night duty had either retired to the boat house to play poker or headed off to Monticello for pizza, Dan lay on his cot in his cabin, remembering the way Rebecca had looked soaking wet.

He'd seen her wet before, lying on the deep-water raft in a swimsuit, but that was different. That time she'd been cool and reserved; this time she'd been surprised and bristling with emotion—and fully clothed.

Closing his eyes, he pictured her breasts, high and taut as the water plastered her shirt against her flesh. He pictured the delectable points of her nipples, and the flatness of her belly and the spot, just above her belt, where the fabric sank in, hinting at her navel.

He thought about her hair, darkened from the water, and her eyes, flashing silver with anger.

If he couldn't have the kind of passion he wanted, he'd take whatever passion he could get. Anger was better than nothing.

The Hawks had had fun tonight. Dan assumed they'd have fun when—*if*—Rebecca and her Chippies reciprocated. Dan hoped they would. The more he could engage Rebecca in Silver Lake's special brand of summer fun, the more connected he would feel to her.

He already knew she was moving away from her father and her ex-fiancé and the properly decorous world they represented. Dan couldn't help thinking that if she was moving away from them, she had to be moving toward him. And that was the sweetest triumph of all.

DAN'S BOYS SPECULATED among themselves on what ghastly fate might be awaiting them inside the screened double door of the Camp Chippewa rec hall. As it turned out, their reception at the social was worse than ghastly.

The Chippies, every single one of them, were dressed to kill.

No chaste white Chippewa shirts this week. The social's hostesses were dressed in all manner of apparel—none demure. Their hair was teased, curled, moussed and adorned with flirty ribbons and bows. They wore droopy earrings and glittering bangles. They smelled of perfume.

Intimidated by the sight of all that nubile beauty lying in wait for them, a few of the boys groaned. Adam Kember was far from intimidated. "Get 'em while they're hot!" he urged his comrades.

"Uh, Adam . . ." Dan clamped his hand around the boy's upper arm. "Adam, I don't want any nonsense, understand?"

"Nonsense?" the boy exclaimed with wide-eyed innocence. *"Moi?"*

Dan took note of the boy's carefully gelled hair, the leather necklace, the superfluous shaving nicks. "This is a dance, not an orgy."

"Did you see the way those babes are dressed?"

"I don't care how they're dressed. I want you to treat them with respect."

"Oh, sure," Adam vowed. "I'll respect them in the morning."

"Adam." Dan knew he was overreacting. Adam was only pulling his leg. If Dan wasn't able to take Adam's bawdy sense of humor in stride, it was because...because he had a feeling his boys were about to be bushwhacked. Rebecca's Chippies—and, he assumed, their leader—were responding to last Wednesday's naval battle with weapons that should have been outlawed by the Geneva Convention.

"Hey, I'll be good," Adam promised. "There's only one babe I'm planning to respect, anyway." He shrugged off Dan's hand and entered the building, shouting, "Stephanie Glynn, light of my life and perfect squeeze—where are you?"

Adam might or might not be good, but he'd be fine. Dan was the one who would wind up surrendering to this Chippewa sneak attack—if Rebecca was a part of it.

Inhaling deeply for courage, he entered the reception hall. He searched the crowd for Rebecca. He didn't see her—until he closed his eyes and saw her wet and enraged on the shoreline, with her clothing pasted to every feminine curve. That image was supplanted by another, more pensive image of her seated beside him in the restaurant booth, momentarily lost in thought, her eyes not hard and metallic but a soft, cloudy gray. He recalled her foot swinging against his shin and her voice, hushed and intense: *Don't simplify my life.*

All right, Dan thought, opening his eyes once more. He wouldn't simplify it. He'd complicate the hell out of it, just as much as she was complicating his life. Once they'd gotten complicated enough, they'd figure out the simplest solution and go for it. No more rivalries and haunting visions, just some good old-fashioned summer fun. And at the end of August she could go home and marry her nice arrogant twit of a boyfriend, if that was what she wanted.

It seemed simple enough to Dan.

But then he spotted her, wending her way across the room to him, and nothing seemed simple at all.

No virtuous white Camp Chippewa shirt for her tonight, either. She had on a fuzzy cream-colored sweater with an enticing scoop neck, a short denim skirt and a pair of sandals made of crisscrossing brown straps, just as tantalizing as the red sandals he'd already grown to know and love. Her jewelry—plain gold hoop earrings and a dainty gold chain around her throat—was less flamboyant than that of her campers, but somehow more alluring. Her hair was pinned back from her face with gold barrettes.

As she drew closer, he took note of the gray shadow and liner enhancing her eyes, the hint of pink along her cheekbones, the sheen of rosy gloss darkening her lips. Closer yet, he inhaled her scent, not flowery perfume or macho musk but baby powder.

On her, it was the most erotic smell he could imagine.

He managed a weak smile. "Is this your revenge?"

She gave him an ingenuous look. "My revenge?"

"You let the girls dress tarty tonight."

"Oh." She surveyed the room and laughed. "I told them we could try it this week, when we were on our home turf, and see if it turned the manly men of Mohawk into salivating beasts."

"I see. And what's your excuse?"

"*My* excuse?"

"Why are you dressed up tonight?"

"Me?" She glanced down at herself, as if she couldn't remember what she had on. "This isn't dressed up, Dan. This is just an old sweater and a blue-jeans skirt."

He could argue that her "old sweater" was dangerously soft and inviting, and that her "blue-jeans skirt" was cut short enough to undermine his equilibrium. But why waste time arguing when he could be dancing with her? He drew her out onto the dance floor and into his arms.

She didn't resist his embrace the way she had last week. She didn't exactly snuggle up to him, didn't hurl herself at him, but she didn't stand stiffly, as if she had a broom handle shoved down the back of her sweater. Her smile spoke of nothing but affection.

"All right, I give up," he said, splaying his fingers out against the small of her back and relishing the graceful slope of her waist. "What are you up to?"

Her smile grew suspiciously sweet. "What makes you think I'm up to anything?"

"Last time I saw you, you looked like you wanted to eat me for breakfast."

"Last time you saw me, I was soaking wet and chilly and not very happy about it," she reminded him, her smile taking on an even more ominous quality. "I can assure you, though, I would never want to eat you."

Merely contemplating what she'd just said caused a taut heat to ignite in the pit of his stomach. It made him want to pull her closer to himself, but he didn't dare. "I can't say I feel the same way about you," he murmured.

Her face turned bright red. "You're disgusting."

He contemplated arguing that there was nothing the least bit disgusting about his suggestion, but he decided it would be far more effective to demonstrate the pleasures of that particular activity than to discuss it. And now was not the time to demonstrate it—or even think about it, as the tension in his stomach crept lower and intensified.

"Okay, let's start all over again," he resolved. "You're looking beautiful this evening."

Her blush faded. "Thank you."

"And I appreciate the fact that you and your girls aren't holding a grudge."

"Of course we aren't," she declared loftily. "We're much too mature for that."

"Of course," he echoed, grinning. He decided to pull her closer, after all, tightening his arms around her and urging her head against his shoulder.

Once again she accepted his embrace without surrendering fully to it. Her cheek rested against him, and her breath brushed the underside of his jaw. He wondered if she had any idea of the effect she was having on him.

To make certain she did, he pulled her closer yet, letting his arm span her narrow waist in back and allowing his hips to slide against hers.

She started slightly, then relaxed and sighed. And kept dancing with him.

A smile whispered across his lips. She definitely wasn't holding a grudge. If all things were possible, he knew exactly what he would want for breakfast.

SHE HAD DECIDED to steer clear of men this summer, hadn't she? She had decided that, after the debacle with Wallace, she wasn't going to get close to anyone for a while.

But this dance with Dan was nothing if not close.

She ought to be objecting to how tightly he was holding her, to the way he was rocking his hips against her, the way he was informing her, in unmistakable terms, of his desire for her. Every time his hips came in contact with hers, her body temperature shot up another few degrees.

Nothing could justify the way she was cuddling against Dan—and the way it was making her feel. Not even the knowledge that at this very moment Maggie and Lisa were emptying dozens of feather pillows across the floors of Camp Mohawk's shower house and administration building.

One tune segued into the next. All around her the air was thick with hormones and violet light from the colored bulbs. A fast song came on, but Dan didn't release her. He continued holding her, moving his fingertips lightly against the hollow of her back and tucking her right hand between his warm body and hers.

"Aren't we supposed to be setting an example?" she murmured, noticing that too many of the campers around them were continuing to dance slowly to the lively Beach Boys song.

"We *are* setting an example," Dan answered, glancing around.

"The wrong example."

"Hey, come on. They're thirteen and fourteen. Nothing's going to happen."

"If you're a high school teacher, you should know better than to believe that," she scolded, drawing back from him.

He grinned. "I always know better. That doesn't keep me from hoping for the best."

"Look, Dan . . ." She sighed. No matter how marvelous she'd felt in his arms, she owed him her honesty. She wasn't in the market for a love affair. If by dancing so close to him she had led him on, she ought to lead him off, right away.

On the other hand, she didn't want to tell him to stop thinking things he might not have been thinking in the first place.

"We shouldn't dance like that anymore," she said weakly.

"You can't get pregnant from dancing."

Obviously he *had* been thinking what she'd been thinking. "Pregnancy is the least of my concerns right now."

"In that case," he said slyly, "let's go find a bed."

"Dan. I'm being serious." Yet a smile tickled her lips.

"Okay," he agreed, effecting a somber expression that was as funny as it was phony. "Let's be serious. You don't want to dance with me? I can handle it. See? My jeans are fitting me better already."

She didn't want to see. She didn't want to think about it. To her great relief, she didn't have to. One of the senior-girls' counselors approached with the news that the popcorn bowls were nearly empty.

"I'll get some more from the kitchen," Rebecca said at once.

Dan fell into step beside her as she started toward the door. "I'll help you."

"Popcorn isn't heavy. I can get it myself."

"I'll get another case of soda while we're there."

Rebecca relented.

"Say thank you."

She shot him a warning look. "Don't push your luck."

The air outside the recreation hall was considerably cooler than the air inside. Rebecca was grateful; she needed to cool off in every way. She inhaled the pine-laced night air, craned her neck to admire the first stars piercing the sky and welcomed the bucolic sounds of crickets and whispering leaves after the dense, atmospheric dance music inside the building.

Dan ambled along the path beside her, making no move to touch her. Last week, when they'd strolled through Camp Mohawk, she'd hooked her hand through the bend in his elbow. She was wise enough not to initiate any contact this week. Not after the way he'd held her inside the recreation hall. Not after the way she'd felt when he had.

"So," he said as they entered the spacious white clapboard building that housed Chippewa's dining room. "I can see why you don't call it a mess hall. The well-bred young Chippies probably eat off porcelain in here."

Rebecca gestured toward the Formica-topped circular tables and folding metal chairs. "You don't have to eat off porcelain to use good manners."

"Meaning, your girls don't toss spaghetti over the rafters."

"Meaning, our dining room hasn't got exposed rafters," she corrected him, glancing up at the ceiling.

They wove among the tables in the shadowy room to the kitchen door at the far end. Once inside, Rebecca switched on the light. She went directly around one of the work counters to the pantry. "There's a case of soda in the refrigerator on the left," she called over her shoulder as she marched down a narrow shelf-lined aisle to the snack-food area.

"I'll get it later," Dan murmured, much too close.

She jumped and spun around. He was right behind her.

"Dan," she whispered. She'd meant to say "Don't," and she'd meant to yell, not whisper. But as he closed in on her between the tall shelves of cereal and flour, cans of fruit and tins of spices, all she could think of was that she wanted this. She wanted him.

He must have read her want in her eyes, in her posture, in the upward tilt of her chin and the expectant parting of her lips. Without hesitation, without asking permission, without a word or a sigh, he cupped his hands around her cheeks and angled her face to receive his kiss.

It was everything she had known it would be, and it was like nothing she'd ever known. His lips were warm and sweet, surprisingly gentle as they stroked hers, brushed hers, nipped and pressed and slid over hers and then finally covered them, coaxing them farther apart.

If only he would force things, if only he were coercive, she would have a reason to back away and slap his face. But his devastating gentleness overpowered her as no show of force could have. With each quiet caress of his lips, each teasing sweep of his tongue along the surface of her teeth, she felt the bones in her legs become a little softer, her heartbeat a little quicker, her balance just a bit more precarious. Damn him for undermining her with tenderness!

Her knees felt rubbery, and she groped for the shelf nearest her, seeking something to hang on to. She accidentally knocked over an open box of Cheerios, and a cascade spilled down along her arms and onto her bare toes. Dan caught her hand in his and guided it to his waist, then brought his other arm around her and hauled her against him.

The instant her body collided with his, his gentle patience vanished. His tongue surged against hers, and they groaned in unison. Turning so he could rest his back against one of the upright shelf supports, he dislodged a soup can with his elbow and set a dozen more cans spilling off the shelf. The racket only inspired him to deepen the kiss.

Rebecca leaned against him as he leaned against the shelf, lifting her arms to circle his neck. He played his tongue over hers, under hers, all around, filling her mouth and then drawing back to trace the edge of her teeth. He bent his leg until he could wedge it between her thighs, beneath the hem of her skirt; he slid his hands down to her hips, hiked her skirt an inch higher and held her tightly against his sleekly muscled thigh. A jumbo box of rigatoni tumbled to the floor.

She had to stop him. She had to stop herself. Somewhere not far away, one hundred young adolescents were starving for popcorn.

But Rebecca had a different kind of hunger, one so profound and pervasive she hadn't even been aware of it until Dan had taken her mouth with his. There was excitement in this kiss; there was competition in it; there was anger and embattlement and, lord help her, so much arousal her legs began to tremble around his and her body began to melt into an urgent, pulsing, humid mass of sensation. It had nothing to do with water fights—and everything to do with them. It had nothing to do with summer fun and games—and everything, everything to do with them.

His fingers arched around her bottom. She gasped and he pulled her higher, against the hard bulge beneath the fly of his jeans. "Rebecca," he whispered, his lips rubbing hers with each devastating syllable. "Becky...God, you feel so good...."

Another box of rigatoni came crashing down, bouncing off her instep.

He shifted, arched against her, rearranged himself so her breasts were crushed in the firm wall of his chest. He kissed her cheeks, her brow, and she grazed along the harsh edge of his chin. He rolled his head back, and she kissed lower, under his jaw. A stack of prefolded paper napkins blizzarded down around them.

"We're making a mess in here," she murmured, unable to keep from running her fingertips along his broad shoulders.

"I like making messes with you." He slid his hands up to her waist, then higher, along the outer edge of her rib cage.

She hugged him tightly, refusing him the space he needed to bring his hands forward. If he touched her breasts, it would be too late. She was so aroused, so insanely, carnally intoxicated that if this thing went any farther she would be undone.

But she couldn't bring herself to let go of him, either.

She had never reacted to a kiss so wildly, so wantonly. Not with Wallace, not with anyone. She had always thought she was basically a cool-headed, cool-blooded woman. She'd gotten her thrills from teaching an eleven-year-old from the reservation how to multiply fractions, or teaching a city slicker from Boston how to walk across a gorge on a rope bridge in northern Maine. She'd gotten her greatest thrills from sleeping under the stars.

Now the stars were inside her, bursting, scattering, shooting along her nerve endings and illuminating her soul.

This was definitely a mess.

Unnerved, she inhaled deeply and averted her gaze so she was no longer viewing Dan. She couldn't bear to look at his sensuous mouth, his lazy-lidded eyes, which were more blue than green tonight, his sturdy jaw and his athletic chest and his shoulders, so strong and rugged she began to understand what the phrase "manly man" really meant.

"Why don't you stack those on the shelf?" she said, waving vaguely at the red-and-white soup cans scattered along the aisle, trying to ignore the uncharacteristic huskiness in her voice. "I'll go get a broom."

Dan pinched the tip of her chin between his thumb and forefinger and turned her face back to his. He must have sensed her uneasiness. "What's wrong?"

She let out a long breath, exasperated that he'd felt it necessary to ask. "I'm not looking for a romance, Dan. You know that. I just broke up with Wallace, I'm under all sorts of pressure from my family, I don't know what's going on in my life and . . . and there are Cheerios all over the floor."

"Oh, yeah, the Cheerios. I tell ya, just when you think nothing else can happen, boom! There go the Cheerios."

"Please, Dan." She'd meant to sound stern, but she sounded only plaintive. Apparently the plea in her voice softened something inside him, because he let go of her and straightened up, allowing her to back away from him.

"Okay. So you just broke up with Wallace. What does that have to do with us?"

"I don't want to start anything with you."

He laughed and plucked a paper napkin from where it had caught on the pocket of her skirt. "Becky, my love, you started something with me the day you turned a hundred glasses full of water upside down in my mess hall."

"Oh, is that what's going on here?" she snapped, suddenly feeling very raw and vulnerable. "Was this kiss part of the ongoing war between Mohawk and Chippewa? Is that it? Pretty crummy tactics, if you ask me."

He grabbed her arm and dragged her back to him. When her face was an inch from his, he said, "What's going on here is that you and I want each other."

"Speak for yourself, Dan. I'm still recuperating from—"

"Forget about Wallace, forget about recuperating, forget about Daddy and his wine list. If you can look me in the eye and tell me you honestly don't feel any attraction to me, say it and I'll never touch you again."

"Promise?"

"Promise."

She imagined a future in which Dan Macklin never touched her again. It was an appallingly dreary thought. She looked him in the eye, and her honesty lay in her silence.

Satisfied, he grinned, loosened his hold and bent over to gather up the soup cans.

She stared at him for a moment, at the powerful arch of his back, the tantalizing contours of his hips, the economical motions of his hands. His shiny brown hair covering his collar. The paler silken hair covering his forearms. His bony wrists. His blunt fingers.

She'd lost this round. As a matter of fact, feather pillows or no feather pillows, she had the unsettling feeling that she'd lost the entire war.

And for the life of her, she didn't know what she was going to do about it.

Chapter Seven

"Dan Macklin is on the phone."

Rebecca glanced toward the doorway of her office, where her secretary hovered. Through the open windows the high-pitched voices of girls playing capture-the-flag floated in on a river of hot, humid air. The desktop fan Rebecca had set up on one corner of her desk did little more than ruffle the papers on her blotter. She was sticky and sweaty and generally in a lousy mood—and the weather was the least of it.

Ever since last Saturday night...

No. She didn't want to think about that. She wanted to make reservations for extra buses for the all-camp trip to see *Peter Pan*. She wanted to review the kitchen inventory and budget. She wanted to write a letter to Samantha Kaye's parents reassuring them that the X rays were all negative and that Samantha was only bruised when she'd fallen out of the tree she shouldn't have been climbing in the first place.

She didn't want to think about the way she'd felt in Dan Macklin's arms, the way her mouth had fused with his and her legs had wrapped around his and her heart had drummed in an unmistakable rhythm, echoing deep within her soul. She didn't want to think about Dan at all.

She certainly didn't want to talk to him.

"I'm not in," she told Kelly.

Kelly nodded, pivoted on her sneakered heel and returned to her office next door to Rebecca's. Ignoring the inventory lists spread across her desk, Rebecca stared at the buttons on her phone. One flashed on and off, signaling that someone was on hold. The light became constant as Kelly picked up her extension in the neighboring office. Then it started to flash again.

Rebecca braced herself for Kelly's return. "He says it's about the water Olympics."

Rebecca grimaced. "Tell him Maggie Tyrell is in charge of that. He can work it out with her."

Kelly nodded again, rotated with a rubber-soled squeak and jogged back to her own office. Rebecca once again watched the phone button, from flashing to solidly on to solidly off.

"Coward," she reproached herself. As if it were cowardly to want to hang on to her mental health. As if there were something inherently gutless in choosing to steer clear of men for a few months. As if self-preservation was a bad thing.

Back at the beginning of the summer, she had wanted to avoid Dan because he annoyed her. Now she wanted to avoid him because he scared her. Really, it wasn't such a big difference, was it?

"He asked me to give you a message," Kelly reported, reappearing in the doorway.

Gritting her teeth, Rebecca looked up expectantly.

Kelly looked mildly embarrassed. "He said...I hope I can get this right. He said to tell you, *'Braaauk! Braaauk!'"* she crowed, a reasonable simulation of a chicken clucking.

Rebecca groaned. "The next time you talk to him, tell him I said, *'Hee-haw, hee-haw.'"*

"I'd just as soon stay out of it," Kelly declared, shaking her head and holding her hands up. "If you guys want to revert to your animal nature, that's your business."

One thing Rebecca *didn't* want was to revert to her animal nature. That was Dan's style, not hers—although maybe it was contagious. He was an ass—and there she was, braying like one.

His resemblance to certain lower mammals wasn't what troubled Rebecca. Rather, it was that she had never responded to a man the way she'd responded to Dan Macklin. She didn't like the effect he had on her. She didn't like the way thoughts of him haunted her, overheated her, made her achy and itchy and temperamental.

She was Rebecca Pruitt, blue of blood and pure of heart, educator and role model. She was Rebecca Pruitt, head of the Chippewas, leader of a summer tribe of warrior-campers. And she resented the fact that merely thinking about Dan made her want to ditch all her responsibilities and have fun.

Dirty fun.

She didn't like any of it at all.

THE SHOP WAS on the outskirts of Bethel. A quarter-century ago, Bethel had been the site of the Wood-stock Festival. While very few remnants of the region's former glory remained in the area, just down the road from Max Yasgur's farm stood a "head shop" run by a sentimental old-timer.

The shop contained all sorts of funky artifacts of that bygone era: blown-glass water pipes, incense burners, Day-Glo posters and black lights. Lava lamps, tarot cards, peace-sign necklaces ... and, Dan hoped, feathers.

It had taken days to clean the linty feathers from Camp Mohawk. Rebecca's henchwomen—whoever they were—had even strewn them across the latrine benches. A week later Dan was still finding curlicues of white down in unlikely places.

It was a magnificent prank, the sort of stunt that elevated Rebecca immeasurably in his esteem. He'd tried to talk to her several times during the week to compliment her on her fiendish inspiration, but she'd refused his calls.

Perhaps she thought he wanted to discuss something else. Perhaps he did. Perhaps he wanted to talk about the fact that for a few astonishing minutes in Chippewa's pantry they had experienced something akin to spontaneous combustion, and he wanted to find out when they could get together again and combust some more.

But she didn't want to talk to him. Indeed, she was so adamant that she wasn't on the Camp Chippewa bus Friday evening, accompanying her senior girls around the lake to Mohawk for their weekly social.

Aggressive action was called for. After asking Jimmy Angelini to supervise the dance, Dan had set out for the head shop in Bethel. He was prepared to go after her, if that was what it took. But first he had to arm himself.

Ignoring the monotonous sitar music, he wandered through the shop until he found what he was looking for: long-stemmed peacock feathers.

The social had just ended by the time he got back to Mohawk. A stream of Chippies trickled slowly along the path to the bus, a few of them escorted by Hawks. Adam Kember and his beloved Stephanie lagged behind the rest of the campers, their arms looped around each other so that their hips smashed together with every other step. He was whispering into her ear, and she was giggling. As they hobbled past Dan in their lopsided Siamese-twin gait, he caught a whiff of musk cologne so strong he nearly gagged.

He remained at Mohawk long enough to wave off the Chippewa bus and get his own boys more or less settled in their bunks. Then he journeyed through the woods to his cabin, checked his reflection in the mirror, splashed a considerably more subtle after-shave onto his cheeks and headed for the boat dock. The air was mild and dry; the moon aimed a fat white beam of light down onto the earth, as if it were God's flashlight.

Dan dragged a canoe down to the water's edge, set the bouquet of peacock feathers gently on the seat in front of him and shoved off. Within a few minutes he reached the pebbly stretch of shoreline near Rebecca's cabin.

As he prowled up the path, he saw two bright rectangles—her windows, illuminated with interior light. An auspicious sign: she was awake. Not that he'd have any objection to waking her up if she weren't, but *she'd* probably object to that.

He climbed up her front steps, raked his fingers through his hair to smooth it down, chastised himself for acting like a certain horny, moony camper of his and rapped his knuckles against the rough-hewn wooden door.

"Who's there?" she called from inside.

"A manly man," he answered.

A long silence ensued. Finally, when he was beginning to scour the surrounding forest for a stick that might serve as a battering ram, she opened the door.

She had on a polo shirt and jeans. No makeup, no fancy barrettes or earrings or sexy sandals. Her face was freshly scrubbed, her hair still damp from a shampoo. Her feet were bare.

She avoided meeting his gaze as effectively as she'd avoided speaking with him all week. Her eyes focused on something behind him, the spot on the ground where he'd come upon a skunk the last time he'd been up this way.

Maybe she thought *he* was a skunk.

"I brought you these," he said, presenting her with the tissue-wrapped bouquet.

She lifted her gaze to his chin and accepted his gift. Folding back the ends of the tissue, she discovered the brilliant blue feathers inside. "Oh, my," she murmured, then laughed.

Relief swarmed through him, relief that she could find humor in the situation, and something more—an organic, erotic pleasure at the sound of her laughter. "Better put them in water before they wilt," he advised, peering past her into the cabin.

Apparently she suspected him of wanting to come in—which, of course, was exactly what he wanted. She set the feathers on a table near the door and then came outside, closing the door firmly behind her.

It was a mighty clear hint, but he refused to become discouraged. At least she wasn't chasing him back to the canoe. Instead, she dropped down to sit on the front step and gestured for him to take a seat next to her.

Neither of them spoke for a minute. He gazed at her feet, still amazed at how small they were. "So," he said, pretending he wasn't the least bit turned on by her nearness, her fresh-scrubbed beauty. "How was your week?"

"Fine," she said blandly.

Her shoulder was close to his. He could bump his shoulder against hers and make it appear accidental. He could bump her shoulder, and brush her knee with his, and then lift her onto his lap and bury his lips between the soft swells of her breasts....

He took a deep breath and shoved his libido back into a safe corner of his brain. "It must have been a whole lot of fun shunning me," he remarked.

"Oh, it was," she assured him. "It was one of the highlights of my life."

He chuckled. His peripheral vision picked up her slight smile. "You know, we had something going there for a few minutes last week. I mean, maybe to you it was run of the mill, but to me it was pretty damned exciting.''

"If this is what you came here to talk about—"

"It's exactly what I came here to talk about." He shifted on the step, angling his body to face her. When she stubbornly stared at her knees, he cupped his hand under her chin and tilted her head up.

Her eyes flashed with silvery light. "Don't do this."

"Do what?"

"Pressure me. I don't want to get involved with you."

"Isn't it a little too late to be worrying about that?"

Even with his hand curved around her chin, she evaded his gaze, darting her eyes from the door to the woods to her knees once more. "All right, I'll admit fate threw us together. We've got to share this lake for the summer. We've got to have weekly socials and the water Olympics—"

"And pillow talk?"

She blinked. He noticed a muscle flutter in her jaw, but she maintained a blank expression. "Pillow talk?"

"The feathers. They were from pillows, weren't they?"

Her eyes darted some more. "Look, if you want to get even with me, okay. Retaliate. Just get it over with, and then we can call off the war. I don't think I—"

"It isn't war, Rebecca, and it isn't something we've got to get over with. This is fun, lady. This is summertime. I mean, I'm kind of crazy about you, and here you are, communicating with me through the medium of pillows. What am I supposed to think?"

"I'm telling you what to think—I don't want to get involved with you."

Dan wasn't actually looking for an involvement himself. But he resented the finality in Rebecca's tone. "Why not?" he challenged.

"For one thing, I'm recuperating from my broken engagement. For another, you're a bum."

"Hmm." He weighed her accusation. "Have you spoken to Chuck lately?"

She appeared startled by the apparent change in topic. "Why do you ask?"

"His wife bought him a treadmill."

Still bewildered, she nodded.

"The idea is, his heart fell apart, and he's got to exercise to heal it and build up his strength. Now, maybe you're recuperating from this so-called engagement of yours—although it seems to me you're lucky to have gotten out of it. But assuming the arrogant twit broke your heart, the best way to recuperate is to get some exercise and give the old ticker a good, solid workout."

"Fine. I'll buy a treadmill."

He laughed. Her feisty spirit turned him on even more than her toes. And her breasts. And her flaxen hair and her starlit eyes. "I told you last week, all you've got to do is tell me you don't want me to touch you, and I won't."

"This has nothing to do with what I want," she snapped, the wry humor gone from her voice, replaced by frustration. "It has to do with staying sane."

"Sanity is a state of mind," he reminded her. "If you want to keep your mind out of it, be my guest.

Your heart, too. I could be happy with access to other parts of your anatomy.''

"I repeat, you're a bum."

"So tell me not to touch you ever again."

She glared at him for a moment, then turned from him and sighed. "Go away, Dan."

"Tell me."

She turned even farther from him. He noticed the shiver that seized her spine, and then the defeat in her slumping shoulders. Lying didn't come naturally to Rebecca, and for her to speak those words would have been a lie.

He arched his hand over her shoulder. It was as if a switch were located there; she suddenly came alive, rotating back to him, swinging her arms around him, opening to him as he covered her lips with his.

God, but she tasted sweet, her mouth all heat and texture, her tongue welcoming his in an explosive reunion. Energy filled him, hunger, lust, greed, all of it spinning through his body before it gathered in his groin and begged for release.

He stroked his hands through her hair and down her back, again and again until she shuddered and moaned—either in protest or encouragement, he didn't know. He didn't care. When his hand reached her waist, he slid it under the edge of her shirt and up again.

She wasn't wearing a bra.

His fingers roved across the smooth expanse of her back, alluringly graceful and silky smooth. He brought his hand forward, and she moaned again, splayed her fingers around his forearm ... and didn't push him away.

Her breast was round, supple, hot, fitting in the curve of his palm, swelling against him. He traced the inflamed nipple, tweaked it, tugged it between his thumb and forefinger until she was whimpering, arching her back and shifting her hips in a restless way that reminded him of his own blissful discomfort.

Her lips continued to mold to his, her tongue to rub and jab his, her breath to stoke the desire burning inside him. His lungs hurt; his hips ached; the muscles in his thighs strained.

"Let's go inside," he whispered, his voice a hoarse rasp in the moon-filled night.

"No." The single word came out on a desperate sob. She pushed against his arm, forcing him to withdraw.

He waited until they'd both caught their breaths before speaking. "Okay, I get the message. You really don't want me to touch you."

She cringed, then shook her head and smoothed out her shirt. "It's not that, Dan. I mean ... it's obvious that I ... I'm not just saying—"

"Full sentences, please."

She shot him an irritated look, saw the smile on his face and relaxed. "Oh, Dan ... What can I say? Everything's just so ... so weird. It's summer. It's a special time. Silver Lake is a special place. Everything seems distorted here, blown out of proportion. Maybe it's because we're only going to be here until the end of August. I don't know, I can't explain it. I just don't trust my emotions, okay?"

"Emotions?" he bellowed in exaggerated horror. "I thought we were talking about sex. What do emotions have to do with it?"

She gave him a lethal stare.

He chuckled, arched his arm around her and drew her against his shoulder. "Lighten up, Becky. You're right—it's a special time and a special place. Why can't we just have some special fun and leave it at that?"

"That would be irresponsible."

"Who says you've got to be responsible every minute of every day? It's summertime, Rebecca. Time for fun. We could have a fantastic time together, and then kiss each other goodbye at the end of August."

She sighed once more, her midriff rising and falling beneath his arm. "I don't think I can do that."

"What's the alternative? Exchanging vows with the arrogant twit? Hey, you can still do that in September. As a matter of fact, if that's what you're going to do, you really ought to have some fun now, while you can. One final fling. Your last chance. A whirlwind summer affair, and then you can grow up and be responsible. It sounds like a good plan to me."

"I'm sure it does."

"It sounds good to you, too."

"It sounds incredibly brainless."

"And you sound like the most arrogant twit of all."

"Thanks a heap." A doleful laugh escaped her. "You'd better go before you really mess me up."

"Is that what I'm doing? Messing you up?" For some reason the thought filled him with pride.

"Go back to Mohawk, Dan."

Actually he wouldn't mind leaving now, full of confidence that while he hadn't achieved a full victory he'd accomplished a great deal. He'd *messed her up.* Life was looking rosy.

"Okay," he said with a spurious show of reluctance. He stood, hitched his jeans and shrugged his shoulders to loosen them. Then he gripped Rebecca's slender wrists and pulled her to her feet. "Lucky for me I've got that life-size inflatable doll waiting for me back in my cabin."

"And you'll have no trouble blowing her up, given all the hot air you're full of."

He dropped a light kiss on her forehead, then leaned away and grinned at her. "Ever hear the expression, 'mixed signals'?"

"Ever hear the expression, 'Go home'?"

He took a step backward toward the path. "I'm not going to keep calling you and getting put off," he warned.

"Fine. Don't call."

"I mean it, Rebecca. You call me."

"Have fun with your doll."

"You know you crave me as much as I crave you."

"I crave my sanity more than I crave you, Dan. Go home."

"Call me," he said, then turned and strode down the path to the canoe. He climbed in, pushed off and paddled into the center of the lake.

Reaching over the gunwale, he cupped his hands full of cold, clear water and doused his face. And doused it again, and then again, praying for it to cool him off.

He found, to his delight and his dismay, that his longing for Rebecca Pruitt was impossible to wash away.

HOURS LATER, still lying awake in bed, she thought about what she'd turned her back on when she'd broken up with Wallace. Security. Stability. Safety.

Lord, but that sounded dull. It shouldn't; there was nothing wrong with desiring those things. Surely it wasn't a sin to want a little continuity in one's life, a little commitment, a little responsibility.

She fingered the tapered edges of the peacock feathers in her hand, tracing the smooth arc on one side to where it met the other side in a point. Although she'd turned her light off, she could make out the brilliant turquoise in the moonlight that filtered through her filmy curtains.

Wallace would never have given her peacock feathers.

What was wrong with her, that she could think peacock feathers were more important than safety, security and stability?

Dan Macklin was what was wrong with her.

She wanted him. With a fierceness that transcended logic. With a yearning that overcame rationality. She wanted his mouth on hers again, and his hand on her skin, on her breasts. She wanted his love.

And all he was prepared to give her was fun and feathers.

She wouldn't call him. He was an egotistical son of a gun, more arrogant than any members of the upper-crust elite with whom she socialized in New York.

What could be more arrogant than annihilating her with a kiss and then swaggering off with a smirk on his face?

He was so sure she'd come running after him, so sure she'd call and say, "Please, Dan, please come and see me! You were right! I was wrong! Let's have fun!"

Never in a million years. She wouldn't give him that satisfaction—even if it meant forgoing her own satisfaction.

But as one hour rolled into the next, as the moon drifted past her windows, over the lake and beyond the horizon, she remained where she was, sprawled out across the wrinkled sheets of her cot, staring into the darkness and clinging to her peacock feathers.

Chapter Eight

Dan was counting basketballs in the sports equipment shack when Pete found him. "Got a minute?" the counselor asked.

"Actually," he said, sliding his pencil under the clip of his clipboard and turning to face Pete, "I've got about two and a half minutes." Even though Rebecca had stretched his patience beyond endurance and his temper grew touchier with each hour she didn't call him, he was proud that he could behave with equanimity around his staff. "What can I do for you?"

"Well..." Pete gave Dan a skittish smile. "It's about Adam Kember."

Dan held up his hand. "Wait, let me guess—he wants to rent stag films and show them in the barn during the next 'Saturday Night at the Movies'?"

"Not quite." Pete shifted from one foot to another. Dan had never seen him look so uncomfortable. "He's asked me to buy him some condoms."

"What!"

"He asked me—"

"I heard you. The answer is no."

Dan slammed the clipboard down on a shelf, sending dust motes swirling in the shaft of sunlight that slanted in through the open door. He had dealt with rowdy campers before, randy campers, ribald campers—but this was too much. How dare Adam request condoms when the Head Hawk, nineteen years Adam's senior, couldn't even get the woman of his dreams to give him a phone call?

"I know it's weird, Dan," said Pete, "but—I mean, it's not like I think he's planning to use them. At least not in the way they're intended."

"What, then? He wants to make water balloons out of them?"

"No. I mean, he *is* pretty hung up on that Chippewa girl...."

"And he's fourteen years old, for God's sake."

"Some fourteen-year-olds are precocious."

"Not in my camp, they aren't. When would he even have the opportunity? They live on opposite sides of the lake, and the socials are chaperoned."

"I know, Dan, I know." Pete shuffled his feet some more. "I'm not disagreeing with you or anything, but, like—it's sort of a good thing that he's trying to take a little responsibility before the fact."

"The fact is not going to happen, not here, not now, not this summer, not within my jurisdiction." Dan took Pete's arm and steered him toward the doorway and out of the shack. "Where is the stud?" he asked.

"They're playing baseball."

"Let's go." Dan jogged ahead of Pete up the path to the softball field. He spotted Adam among a crowd of boys swarming in the dugout, shouting obscenities at the pitcher. It was an oddly reassuring scene, the sort of behavior one expected of normal fourteen-year-old boys.

Dan sidled up to the dugout. "How's the game going, guys?" he asked with deceptive nonchalance.

"That pitcher sucks eggs," one of the boys announced.

"We're kickin' butt here," another gloated.

Adam sniffed and squinted into the sunshine. "Don't be nasty, boys. The pitcher can't help it. He was born with the weenie gene."

Dan allowed himself a moment to admire the originality of Adam's insult. Then he called, "Adam, can I talk to you for a minute?"

Adam glanced at his teammates, who looked intrigued. Their fascination fed his ego. "Sure thing," he said, strutting out of the dugout and around the chain-link fence.

Arching his arm casually around the boy's shoulders, Dan ushered him out of earshot of his teammates. "Listen, Adam, I understand you asked Pete to buy some contraceptives for you in town."

"Well..." Adam's cheeks darkened slightly, but he didn't shrink from the question. "I intend to pay him back."

"That's not the point, Adam. The point is you're not going to sleep with Stephanie Glynn. I want that very clear between us."

"But—"

"I don't care what you do at home or at school. At Camp Mohawk, I make the rules. And one of my rules is, no sex." *No sex indeed,* he thought churlishly. That rule ought to have applied only to the campers of Silver Lake, not to the adults. Unfortunately Rebecca Pruitt had her own set of rules, and they seemed to include ignoring the most inflammable case of mutual attraction in the history of intergender relationships.

He mustn't let himself be distracted, though. The issue of the moment was Adam Kember's hyperactive libido, not Dan's.

"The thing is," Adam was saying, "Stephanie Glynn is awesome."

"You'll get no argument from me on that. But that doesn't mean you're going to sleep with her. Do you know what *in loco parentis* means?"

Adam mulled over the phrase. "Something like, 'your parents are crazy'?"

Dan smiled in spite of himself. "It means, when your parents aren't around, I'm the substitute parent and I set the limits. If Stephanie is really special to you, respect her and respect yourself. If it's a summer romance, it's not true love and you don't want to get all tangled up in something as serious as sex. If it *is* true love, it will last. You'll have plenty of time for sex when you're older."

Adam scowled. "My parents would say go for it."

Dan doubted that, but he didn't waste time arguing with Adam. "What your parents would say is irrelevant. At Camp Mohawk, I'm the boss."

Adam dug the toe of his sneaker into the dirt, shaping a small crater. "The thing is, Dan, it wasn't like I was necessarily going to use them, you know? It was more like, you know, what you said. I respect her, and if I show her I'm willing to protect her, it's like a sign of love, you know?''

Dan shrugged. "I understand what you're saying, Adam, but that sort of thing can backfire on you. She could see it as a sign of pressure. And pressuring a woman is the quickest way to turn her off." Although sometimes, he added silently, before she was turned off she could be incredibly turned on.

But then, Rebecca's accusations to the contrary, Dan hadn't really pressured her. Whatever pressure she'd felt had been entirely self-inflicted.

Damn it, he wished she would give in. The pressure *he* was under was keeping him awake nights.

"So, no rubbers, huh," Adam conceded.

Dan shrugged again and patted Adam's shoulder. "Do yourself a favor, Adam—don't grow up faster than you have to. Enjoy being a kid. It doesn't last forever."

Then he turned and stalked down the path to the sports equipment shack, trying to think of some suitable act of vengeance to wreak on Rebecca for her gall in refusing to telephone him. Something really vile, really annoying. Something outlandishly immature.

Who said being a kid didn't last forever?

HE THOUGHT of numerous pranks, but none of them excited him. The depressing fact was, he didn't want to annoy Rebecca. He wanted to make love with her.

After dinner he returned to his office. He couldn't bear the thought of going to his cabin alone, lying in his sagging cot and wrestling with insomnia yet another night. He sat at his desk in the brightly lit room, staring at his blotter, at the insurance forms from the clinic in Monticello where the Velikofsky brothers went for their allergy shots, at the darkness beyond his window, at his silent telephone.

He could call her.

No, he couldn't. What he'd told Adam about pressuring women was true.

Besides, he had a right to expect her to put some effort into their relationship, didn't he? He'd made all the moves so far; all she'd done was moan and clutch him and kiss him wildly and move her wickedly enchanting body against his—and then tell him to go away. Well, Dan Macklin believed in equality between the sexes. It was long past time for Rebecca to make a move.

Except that she obviously wasn't going to.

Cursing, he lifted the phone and started to dial the number for Camp Chippewa's central switchboard. After the third digit he slammed the phone down. Then he lifted it again and dialed a different number.

"Hello?" Chuck DeVore's voice boomed over the wire.

"I'm losing my grip, Chuck," Dan lamented. "Save me."

"*You're* losing *your* grip? Try living on flounder and steamed broccoli for a month and see what happens to your grip. I dream of steak and butter and cream, and I wake up in a sweat."

Dan suffered a pang of sympathy for his friend, then decided that it was more fun feeling sorry for himself. "That harpy across the lake is doing me in."

"Rebecca Pruitt?" Chuck sounded astonished. "She seems like a nice gal. What's she doing to you?"

"She's turning me into a creature of unfulfilled lust."

Chuck laughed. "You've always been a creature of lust."

"Not unfulfilled."

"In other words, she isn't interested in you?"

"She *is*. That's the problem. We've reached a certain point, and she refuses to go any further. She says she's still hung up on her ex-boyfriend, and she doesn't want to get involved with anyone right now. I told her what I want is very uninvolved, but she—"

"Whoa," Chuck silenced him. "Slow down, Danny. Take a deep breath."

Dan did.

"Give her a break. Maybe she *is* hung up on her ex-boyfriend. She's entitled. Why are you giving her a hard time?"

"Because she's giving me a hard time. *Very* hard," he emphasized. Merely thinking about her silvery eyes and pale hair and the warm curve of her breast against his hand brought on the most physical manifestation of the hard time she was giving him.

"She's not the only woman in the Catskills," Chuck reminded him.

"I don't want any other woman."

"Then go after her properly," Chuck advised. "If you want her, romance her. Court her. Take her seriously. Get involved, if she means that much to you. You're thirty-three years old, Dan. By the time I was thirty-three, Irene and I were an old married couple."

"Who said I wanted to marry Rebecca?"

"If she doesn't matter that much to you, then forget about her. If she does..." Chuck's voice drifted off, leaving his meaning clear.

"I don't want to marry her. Frankly, Chuck, what I want is to get over her. She's an obsession, that's all. I want to stop obsessing. You got any suggestions?"

"Why don't you clear out on your next day off?" Chuck obliged. "Take a hike. Go backpacking. Commune with nature or something. Talk to the bugs."

Dan considered. "Yeah, maybe I will. Just get the hell away from her and remember what's important in life."

"The sun, the sky, the trees—"

"Uncomplicated women."

"That's the idea."

Dan smiled. "I miss you, Chuck. How are you feeling?"

"As well as can be expected, given all the bran I've been eating. You know what bran tastes like? Sawdust."

"How much weight have you lost?"

"Ten pounds. Irene can't keep her hands off me."

Dan briefly wondered whether he'd prompt the same response from Rebecca if he ate bran. Or sawdust. Perhaps the stuff acted as an aphrodisiac...?

"Speaking of which, I gotta go," Chuck said. "Gotta get my pulse rate up again."

It wasn't Chuck's pulse rate Dan envied. It was his marriage, his cheerful disposition. Irene might not like camping, but she liked Chuck—and she loved him.

Not that Dan was ready for an involvement or anything like that, not that he was looking for true love,
but... Someday he would have to grow up.

He'd grown up once—long before he should have
had to—and eventually he knew he would grow up
again. There were times—like the present, when he
could imagine himself agreeing to any terms, any
conditions, just to have Rebecca's arms around him
for a night—when growing up seemed like a very real
possibility.

Nah. Not yet. Not for the queen of the arrogant
twits.

He'd rather take a hike.

HE LEFT MIDMORNING Tuesday, clad in khaki shorts,
heavy boots, a T-shirt and his headband. His sleeping
bag and pup tent were tied onto his backpack frame.
If he'd bothered to shave and trim his hair, he would
have resembled a model in an L.L. Bean catalog.

He journeyed north on a trail paralleling the lakeshore, heading for his favorite hideaway on the bluff
above the lake where the blueberries grew wild. Just
beyond the northern border of the camp he found a
fallen oak branch the perfect length to serve as a
walking stick. He extended his legs, took long strides,
inhaled the warm, crisp mountain air and ignored the
skeeters.

Chuck was a wise man, he thought. When in trouble, head for the hills. When unprepared to grow up,
run away. When loneliness threatened, discover the
comforts of solitude.

The farther along the trail Dan hiked, the better he felt. The hell with Rebecca and her hot-and-cold act. Once August ended he would be back in the 'burbs, surrounded by friends, dating and partying and having a grand old time. The hell with Miss Prissy-Sissy Pruitt from the stratosphere of Manhattan society.

Yeah. This was the ticket. Just Dan and the woods. Just Dan and the earth and the endless sky.

By two o'clock the foliage began to thin out, revealing more and more of that endless sky. His canteen was dry, his stomach hollow, but the end of the trail was in sight. Amid the yammering of the birds, the noxious hum of flies and the rustle of leaves, he heard the welcome song of the brook.

He raced toward it, dropped onto his knees and drank straight from the clear current. Then he refilled his canteen, hoisted himself back onto his feet and trampled toward the clearing—

And cursed.

There was a tent pitched on the best spot of the bluff, the perfect spot, *his* spot. Right next to the campfire pit he'd dug and lined with rocks two years ago, beneath the shelter of trees he'd always used.

Someone else had gotten here first. Someone had stolen the solitude he so desperately needed.

If that wasn't bad enough, the tent flaps opened and the owner crawled out: a golden-haired woman with silver eyes, long legs and the most enticing figure Dan had ever had the misfortune to encounter.

She straightened up, saw him and screamed.

Chapter Nine

"What the hell are you doing here?" he shouted from his position across the field, a hundred yards away.

Rebecca took a deep breath and prayed for strength. She had trekked up this trail Maggie had told her about, for the express purpose of avoiding the very man who faced her now.

"What do you mean, what the hell am I doing here?" she retorted, planting her hands on her hips and giving him her fiercest frown. "I'm camping here. It's my day off. I'd suggest you find your own place."

"This is my own place," he argued, approaching her in long, ominous strides. "See that wonderful fireplace pit? Mother Nature didn't leave that there for you. *I* built it."

"It doesn't have your name on it," she snapped. "If you don't hold the deed to this land, you can't kick me off it."

He opened his mouth and shut it. His eyes narrowed on her, smoldering with unleashed rage. Definitely green, she decided—and definitely too hypnotic for her well-being. She lowered her gaze, and it

alighted on his mouth, which proved just as dangerously attractive. His jaw was darkened with a stubble
of beard, and a virile dagger of sweat dampened his
shirt front.

Such a manly man, she thought, then turned away
in disgust.

"Why don't you leave?" she asked.

"What's the matter?" he taunted. "Are you afraid
that if I stay you'll lose control and throw yourself at
me?"

That struck uncomfortably close to the truth. She
turned back to him, raising her chin pugnaciously.
"Don't worry, Dan—I've got more control than you
can bear."

"You sure do," he retorted. "Control is your middle name—Rebecca Control Pruitt."

"Go away."

"That's becoming quite a refrain with you, Becky.
'Go away!'" he singsonged in a kindergartener's
whine. "Don't worry, toots—I'll pitch my tent on the
other side of the field. Far be it from me to want to
corrupt you. I'll just go and be dirty at the other end."

"You do that," she muttered, sounding less deri-
sive than she would have liked. Knowing that he was
on the bluff with her, no matter how far away, unsettled her. If he kissed her again, what would she do?
She couldn't lock him out. Even if he didn't kiss her
again, she would be much too conscious of his nearness.

Today she was too conscious of everything. She'd
had a terrible conversation with her father that morn-

ing—and with Wallace. Now all she wanted was to be alone, to pick berries and tune out the static of her life.

And forget about Dan Macklin.

She reached inside her tent for the mess-kit pot and tramped across the field to where the berry bushes were densest. As she sought the plump berries, she struggled in vain against the temptation to gaze in his direction.

He was pitching his tent. Like his backpack, it was blue. The sack that held his sleeping bag was blue, as well. No doubt his eyes would change from green to blue when he lay down inside. His eyes would be a seductive blue, and his body...

She bit down hard on a berry, as if she were in agony and trying to keep from howling.

She wished she could blame her father for her mood. He'd had no right to spring Wallace on her the way he had. He had called right after breakfast. "I'm in my office right now, and someone just walked in who wants to talk to you."

Before Rebecca could argue, Wallace's voice had come on the line.

She'd gnashed her teeth, steeling herself for whatever he might say. He'd been more devious than she expected; rather than hectoring or cajoling her, he'd announced that a friend of theirs was pregnant. "The baby is due in February. Naturally she's put down a deposit at the Talbot Day School to hold a place open for the child."

"That's insane! How can you hold a place at a school for someone who isn't even born yet?"

"It's better than finding out there's no room in the best schools and you have to send your child to some second-rate place, like Miss Hetheridge's or Mac-Kenzie. If we'd had children, Rebecca, I certainly would have put down in utero deposits for them at Talbot."

If we'd had children... Oh, yes, Wallace had known which button to push. That he could attempt to manipulate her with a reminder of her longing for children proved that she'd been right to end their engagement.

She hated them all: her father and Wallace, and most of all Dan Macklin for nearly convincing her that a breezy, no-strings-attached fun summer fling would be worth the pleasure it brought, even though it wouldn't lead to children or commitments.

Now she hated him even more because she had to share this blueberry field with him.

He was harvesting berries at the other end of the field. It was a big enough area; they could both fill their mess-kit pots without ever bumping into each other.

She felt the force of his presence, though. It hung in the air around her like a scent, like the sun's warmth. It permeated her, infected her, disturbed her equilibrium.

She kept picking berries, hoping the task would keep her from dwelling on Dan and her disastrous love life. After about an hour sweat glued her hair to her face, and her shoulders ached. Her bones clicked and creaked as she straightened up with her heaping pot of berries. She headed down to the brook to rinse her harvest and her face.

The cool water refreshed her. After drenching her face and throat, she washed her berries a handful at a time, dumping them back into the pot once they'd passed inspection. When she hoisted herself to her feet, she felt significantly better.

Until she turned around and found Dan right behind her, holding his own heaping pot of berries.

They glared at each other for a tense, silent minute. Then he spoke. "You did kiss me, you know. I didn't imagine it. You kissed me."

"And I regret it."

"You're a liar."

"That's one thing I'm not," she declared, cradling her pot and stalking past him.

She *did* regret it; of course she did. She regretted that he was so sexy and she was so susceptible. She regretted that she couldn't look into his eyes without feeling an encroaching helplessness. She regretted that a woman as cool and composed as she was, one never given to histrionic passion, dissolved into a mass of steamy yearning whenever Dan got too close, whenever he gave her one of his sensuous smiles, whenever his hand brushed against her.

She wished she had never kissed him. She wished she could promise herself she never would again—but gazing up at him beside the brook had made her wonder how she would find the strength to resist him if he made a pass at her.

The sun had begun to dip below the treetops; the late afternoon was still warm, but with the gathering dusk the air would grow cooler soon.

She changed into warmer clothes, made a campfire and put a foil-wrapped potato among the coals to roast. She was carrying a few more pieces of wood for the fire from her pile beside the tent when she found herself toe-to-toe with Dan.

He, too, had donned jeans and long sleeves. His headband was gone, his face scrubbed although still unshaven. He carried his pot of berries, the rest of his mess kit and the drawstring sack from his sleeping bag. "It would be a waste to build two fires," he said slowly. "I think we ought to act ecologically."

In other words, he wanted to share her fire. Great.

He must have read the skepticism in her face, because he added, "I did construct this pit, don't forget."

"You want to cook here? Go ahead, cook here." She was tempted to make a wisecrack about how he was too lazy to build his own fire, or too inept, but she held her words and engrossed herself in whittling the forked tips of a green stick she'd found for cooking her hot dogs.

Dan opted for silence, as well. Rebecca tried not to follow the sounds he made, but no matter how diligently she strove to ignore him, she remained acutely aware of his every move. Even when she wasn't looking at him she saw him, felt him, sensed his proximity in every cell of her body.

The stick he chose to whittle was much thicker than hers—a good two inches in diameter. Unable to stop herself, she watched as he scraped one end of it clean of bark and dirt with his pocketknife. She wondered why he hadn't found a more suitable stick.

Satisfied with the smooth pale tip he'd fashioned on the stick, he set it aside, emptied some white powder into a pot, added water and stirred it into a pasty dough. He scooped up a bit of the dough, molded it around the end of the stick and then propped the stick on a couple of rocks so the fire's warmth would envelop the dough without burning it.

She didn't want to ask, but she couldn't help herself. "What is that?"

"A dough-boy," he said laconically, tossing a handful of blueberries into a pot, adding a splash of water and a couple of teaspoon-size packets of sugar, mashing the berries with the tines of a fork and balancing the pot on two sturdy sticks that spanned the fire.

Rebecca tried to concentrate on peeling the skin from a hot dog, but curiosity about Dan's cooking gnawed at her. He alternately stirred his blueberry mixture and rotated the stick. "What kind of dough is it?" she asked.

"It's biscuit mix. Add-water-and-stir stuff."

"And it can bake on an open fire?"

"If you make it the right thickness. Too thin, and it burns. Too thick, and it doesn't cook through."

"I see." She impaled her hot dog on her stick and thrust it toward the fire. The sky was turning pink. Shadows played mysteriously across Dan's face, emphasizing the sharp line of his nose, giving his bristle

of beard a smudgy appearance, drawing her attention
to his lips.

Why was she up here alone with him? How could
this be happening? The plan was to stay away from
men for a while, to detach herself from their nonsense.

Yet Dan's knack for camp-fire cookery didn't seem
the least bit nonsensical. Nor did his quiet smile, or his
confidence, or the flourish with which he stirred his
berries and tended to his dough-boy, turning the stick
again and again until the dough was an even tan color.

He removed the stick from the heat and slid off the
dough. It had baked into a cup shape. By the time he'd
spooned some stewed blueberries into the cup, Rebecca's mouth was watering. Not for a hot dog. Not even
for a kiss.

Dan glanced up. Evidently he was able to read her
hunger. After a torturous second, he extended the
dough-boy to her.

"Thank you," she murmured.

"Let it cool off a little first," he warned, taking
another lump of dough and smoothing it around the
tip of the stick.

She held the steaming biscuit in her hand and wrestled with her emotions. That he could whip up such a
treat and then be so generous with it upset her, because it made him likable. She didn't want to like him.

She certainly didn't want to be beholden to him.
"Would you like one of my hot dogs?" she asked,
hoping to settle her debt.

He arranged his dough-boy stick against the rocks
and smiled at her. "I'd love one."

He spoke so simply, so directly, she felt her hostility ebb away. It was all right to like him, after all. As long as he wasn't trying to seduce her, she could like him just fine.

"I only brought one potato," she said apologetically, "but we can share it."

"Or we can pig out on dough-boys and forget the potato."

Rebecca took a bite of her dough-boy and instantly agreed. Warm, sticky berry juice dripped down her fingers, and she licked them off. "This is wonderful. Where did you learn how to make it?"

"Oh, I know all kinds of wonderful things," he said with a sly grin.

Rebecca refused to let his teasing rattle her. She took another bite, caught the juice on her lips with the tip of her tongue and sighed. "I'm sorry."

He shot her a quizzical look. Abashed by his scrutiny, she focused on the hot dog, lowering the stick until the flames lapped at the meat. "About not calling me?" he asked when she didn't elaborate on her apology.

Her embarrassment increased, but she wouldn't retreat. They were alone together on a hilltop, seated beside a roaring fire in the waning light. If ever there was a time to be honest with Dan Macklin, it was now. "About the way I reacted when you showed up this afternoon. I hiked here because I needed some time alone, and when I realized I wasn't alone, I guess I didn't take it very well."

He dismissed her self-reproach with a shrug. "I came up here to be alone, too," he confessed.

Abruptly suspicious, he muttered, "That SOB! I can't believe he'd trick us that way!"

"Who?"

"Chuck DeVore. Did he tell you to come here?"

"No. Maggie Tyrell suggested it."

"Okay," Dan grunted, mollified. "Last night I talked to Chuck, and he told me I ought to spend my day off here. If he'd told you the same thing..."

Nonplussed, Rebecca swallowed the last of her dough-boy. "Do you think he's trying to get us together?"

"I guess not." Dan pulled the dough-boy out of the flames and slid it off the stick. "He happens to think highly of you."

Rebecca was touched. Now that she'd run Camp Chippewa for a few weeks and seen how difficult it was, she was coming to think highly of Chuck. "But he doesn't seem like the matchmaker type."

"I bet if he tried to match you with me, you'd give him an earful."

Rebecca's gaze met Dan's through a ripple of smoke. "Probably," she allowed. "We're an awful match."

Dan laughed. "Obviously. With you it's got to be a fancy rich guy or no one at all."

His remark stung. "Wealth has nothing to do with anything," she claimed. "And if fancy living was important to me, do you think I'd be cooking over an open fire right now? No, Dan—what makes us a bad match is that I'm an adult and you're not."

"Oh." He rubbed his chin thoughtfully, as if that would help him digest her profound observation. "I'm not an adult. Hmm. Coming from someone whose idea of fun is to dump feathers all over a person's office—''

''That was strictly getting even. I wasn't the one who started all that intercamp silliness.''

''I know, I know. I take full credit for it, Rebecca. I would never accuse you of having fun voluntarily.''

''You see? We're a terrible match.''

''Except when we're kissing?'' he proposed, reaching around the fire and taking the hot-dog stick from her. ''Why didn't you call me?''

She watched as he flipped the stick back and forth, giving the wiener a more even cooking. In her mind she flipped her answer back and forth, knowing even as she did that there was only one way to respond to his question: truthfully. ''I don't doubt that we could have fun together, Dan,'' she admitted quietly. ''But I'm not . . . I'm not looking for fun.''

''You don't have to look for it. It's already there. All you have to do is help yourself to it.'' He pulled the hot dog out of the flames, dropped it onto his mess-kit plate and passed the stick back to her for a refill.

''Fun has its place,'' she granted, ''but . . . well, it's just that you're like a little boy, Dan. You think fun is the ultimate goal in life. I don't.''

''What's your ultimate goal?''

She pierced the stick's whittled points through another frankfurter and handed it back to him. ''My ultimate goal? To settle down, eventually. To get married. To have children, if it isn't too late.''

''You've got years and years before you have to worry about it being too late.''

"I'm considered an old maid in my family," she told him. "My sister got married right out of college, my brother right out of law school. And here I am, almost thirty and still single."

"How come you didn't get married right out of college?"

"There were other things I wanted to do."

"And you thought that once you got married, you wouldn't be able to do them?"

The day had lost more light, freeing her to gaze at Dan a bit more openly. She'd never really thought about it, but his question struck home with startling force. It was true; she had always assumed that once she got married she wouldn't be able to light out for the wilderness, to teach Outward Bound classes and sleep beneath the stars. Wallace had established that if they had children, he wouldn't want her taking them camping. Her family had urged her to get all her rebellious outdoorsy impulses out of her system before she settled down.

"I used to be very mature," Dan informed her.

In the twilight Rebecca could see the glint of humor in his eyes. "Quite the manly man, I'll bet."

"I'm still manly," he boasted playfully. His smile faded, though the sparkle remained in his stunning blue-green eyes. "When I was thirteen my father died."

"Oh, Dan—how sad."

"It was a long time ago," he said, dismissing her sympathy. "When it happened, my mother was totally helpless. She was the archetypical full-time traditional housewife. She didn't know how to balance a checkbook. She didn't know how to get her car serviced. My father had always taken care of everything, and when he was gone she didn't know what to do. So I did everything.''

''Everything?''

''I invested his life insurance for her. When she missed a few payments on the mortgage, I went with her to the bank to straighten it out, and from then on I took care of the bills. I made sure my brothers were signed up for Little League and the Boy Scouts on time, and for their S.A.T.s and all that stuff. Money was tight, so I took an after-school job, and I figured out the household budget.'' He twisted the hot-dog stick to cook the other side of the meat. ''When my father died, my mother turned to me and said, 'Dan, you're the man of the family now,' and she was right. I grew up real fast.''

Rebecca absorbed his words, moved not only by what he'd confided but that he was confiding in her at all. She tried to mesh her knowledge of Dan as a cutup with the responsible teenager he'd just described.

To her amazement, Rebecca could envision it. She could see traces of that overwhelmingly responsible young man in Dan.

She felt ashamed of herself, not only for having judged him so harshly but for having never had to face the struggles he had endured. She'd spent so much of her adult life testing herself against Mother Nature and her conservative parents, safe in the knowledge that if she failed, a plush layer of money would cushion her fall. Dan hadn't had to test himself. Life had handed him a formidable test. And he'd aced it.

"So, you see," he continued, handing her the cooked hot dog, "I missed out on being a kid when I was young. That's why I've got to be a kid now."

"I suppose you've earned the right," she said.

"The trouble is, it turns you off."

Unable to meet his gaze, she stared at the dancing yellow flames and nibbled on her hot dog. Around her the night became gilded with moonlight and the sounds of crickets and birds and the burning wood. Her face remained hot from the fire's radiance, but her arms and back grew cool as the summer heat trailed the sun over the western horizon.

She felt Dan's eyes on her. She heard the scrape of his fork against the plate, a muffled gurgle as he took a drink from his canteen.

His statement hung in the air, false yet unchallenged.

"No," she whispered. "The trouble is, it turns me on."

Chapter Ten

The atmosphere grew strangely still. The fire kept burning, the flames flickering, ruffling the air—and yet Rebecca felt somehow immobilized, bound in a tacit understanding with Dan.

He stared at her, his eyes reflecting the firelight, his dark hair loose around his face, his mouth curved in a mystified half smile.

At last the spell relaxed its grip on them both. He shook his head and chuckled. "You are the most contradictory lady I've ever met."

"I'm not contradictory," she argued.

"See? You're contradicting me right now."

She smiled reluctantly. "I'm not contradictory," she repeated. "I'm just confused."

"Well, so am I." He scooped a handful of blueberries out of the pot and popped them into his mouth, one at a time. "Is it your arrogant-twit ex-fiancé who's confusing us, or is it something else?"

"It's me," she admitted, setting down her plate and resting her head in her hands, her elbows propped on her knees. "I've never had to take care of anyone."

Speaking the words compelled her to recognize what a great shortcoming that was.

"You're taking care of, what, nearly two hundred campers and staff at Chippewa?"

"That's not the same thing."

"And you take care of all those students at Piedmont."

"Claremont. And it's not as if their lives are depending on me—"

"And you took care of kids on an Indian reservation."

"I was a schoolteacher, that was all," she asserted, wondering where he'd learned about her work in Cherokee, North Carolina. "I taught fifth grade. That's not the same as keeping a roof over your family's head."

The fire brought out the golden undertones in his complexion. For the first time since she'd met him, she could look at him and not think about his potent handsomeness. He was attractive, of course, but what she saw in his face was friendship, trust, someone as honest and self-aware as she was trying to be. "Maybe the reason I go camping is that it gives me a chance to take care of myself. Everyone's always taken care of me. Except out here." A faint smile skimmed her lips. "At least I don't have to worry about you wanting to take care of me."

"Yeah? Who made you that dough-boy?"

"Excuse me, I stand corrected. I would have starved to death if you hadn't given me that."

"Hey, you ought to be grateful."

"I am," she acknowledged, no longer teasing. "I'm grateful to you for letting me take care of myself."

He swallowed the last of his blueberries, then shifted closer to her. "Why are you afraid to take care of your passionate nature?" he asked.

His voice was so gentle, so unthreatening, she didn't recoil. Her chin still resting in her hands, she tilted her head to peer at him. "I haven't got a passionate nature."

He let out an incredulous laugh. "Are you kidding?"

"I mean it. The couple of times we kissed, Dan— those were anomalies. I'm not usually like that."

"Obviously you've never been kissed by a manly man before."

"Oh, hush." She gave him a playful shove. Before she could withdraw her hand, he captured it in his. The slight movement of his thumb against her palm ignited a tremulous heat in her arm, in her entire body. Maybe she did have a passionate nature—if someone like Dan was willing to liberate it.

"I'm not asking for much," he murmured, evidently sensing her response to the light friction of his thumb. He closed his other hand around hers, enveloping her fingers. "If you want to go home and get married this fall, that's okay. If you want to run off and teach the Aleuts in Alaska, fine with me. We're both confused here, but I think we could simplify a lot of things if you just gave yourself permission to have some fun."

"Dirty fun," she muttered, unnerved by the quivering in her voice.

"Very clean, healthy fun." His thumb continued to stroke her palm while his other hand inched up to her wrist, to her forearm. Slowly, without coercion, he urged her closer to him, closer, until he could slide his arm around her waist and lift her into his lap.

His mouth claimed hers eagerly, hungrily. She accepted his kiss, surrendered to it, triumphed in it—and in her own passionate nature, the existence of which she would never have known if Dan hadn't come into her life.

He wasn't asking for her future, her heart or any of the things she considered essential in a true love affair. He wasn't asking for her love. All he wanted was fun.

Summer was the season for fun, wasn't it? The season for romps, for flings, for bodily delights, for bare feet and whimsy, for kisses that tasted like sweet fruit and skin that smelled of woods and smoke, for a woman like Rebecca to explore the boundaries of clean, healthy fun with a man like Dan Macklin.

This was good, she told herself. This was basic. It had nothing to do with love and everything to do with trust. She trusted Dan.

Ringing her arms around him, she angled her head and deepened the kiss. He groaned and slid his hands down past her hips to her thighs, drawing her legs forward around his waist and pressing her body fully to his. Then he brought his hands back up, tracing her spine to the nape of her neck and weaving his fingers into her hair.

After another prolonged minute, he broke the kiss. "Are you going to stop me this time?" he whispered, still twining his fingers through her hair. His chest pumped against hers, his breathing labored. "I'd rather know before we go too far."

Her respiration was as ragged as his. She felt his abdomen flex against her, felt his arousal, and her breath grew even more erratic.

She tried to assess the logical reasons for stopping this thing before it got out of control. But all she could think of was that her life was much too controlled, and that now, in the early days of August, far from her very controlled existence, it was time to let go.

She lifted her hands from his shoulders, lowered them to the edge of his shirt and pulled it up over his head.

His legs heaved under her, his entire body shifting as he tore off his shirt and then hers. With deft efficiency he undid the clasp of her bra, letting the lacy undergarment fall away.

Rebecca experienced a sudden pang of bashfulness. It wasn't enough that Dan could see her breasts; even worse was that the moths and voles and owls could see her, the trees and shrubs and the moon.

He caught her hands before she could cover herself, and pinned them down at her sides. He seemed transfixed by the amber glow of the fire dancing across her skin. Without releasing her hands, he bowed and kissed the rise of one breast, and then the other, and then the valley between them.

She shivered, not from cold but from the heat his kisses had kindled inside her. She struggled to free her hands, but he refused to let go. She could do nothing but kneel motionless before him as he grazed over her breasts, nipping at one nipple and then the other, rising as high as her collarbone and her throat and then bowing again, kissing, licking, sucking until she let out a sob of frustration.

He pulled back, loosening his grip on her wrists. "Where's your sleeping bag?"

"In the tent," she mumbled, reaching for his warm, inviting chest and groaning as he eluded her. He crawled partway into the tent, dragged out the puffy down-filled bag and sprawled out across it, rolling onto his back and pulling her onto him.

They kissed again, and when she tore her lips from his he didn't restrain her. She explored his chest with her hands, caressing the hard surface of muscle and bone, the wedge of hair that narrowed down to his stomach, the ridge of his ribs and the dark circles of his nipples. She journeyed up to his shoulders, down his arms, over the backs of his hands and across his stomach again, down to his navel, to the edge of his jeans and up once more.

He arched beneath her, and she smiled at the realization that he was as sublimely frustrated now as she had been just a moment ago. If she'd learned anything this summer, it was the joy of retaliation.

"Rebecca," he murmured, arching his hips again as she continued to stroke his chest, as she brushed her lips over the scratchy stubble of his day-old beard, along the underside of his chin, down his sternum and through the matted brown hair to his nipple. She touched it with the tip of her tongue and watched in fascination as it tightened into a point.

She'd never done anything like that before. She'd never taken charge of lovemaking, moving at her own pace, being creative, breathing in the smoky night air, straddling a man and making his nipples hard with her tongue.

She'd never done anything like any of this. But it was summertime and this was fun, and she couldn't possibly wind up more confused afterward than she already was.

Inspired by her own boldness, she wriggled lower, kissing a path down to his navel. A slightly crazed laugh escaped him, causing his abdomen to twitch beneath her in a tickly way that made her laugh, as well. He tucked his hands under her arms and hoisted her back up until he could plant a noisy, exuberant kiss on her lips. "Becky..." His voice emerged on a harsh breath. He skimmed one hand down to the snap of her jeans and popped it open. "Becky...are you protected? I don't have anything with me."

She thought of the pills she'd been taking, at Wallace's insistence, ever since she and he had become engaged. "Of course we'll have children," he had vowed. "As many as you'd like. But we've got to be responsible, Rebecca. We can't just jump into parenthood, can we?"

She had seen no reason why they couldn't, given that everyone—namely her parents and Wallace himself—seemed to think they were a perfect couple. Obviously they *weren't,* though. And for the first time since he had persuaded her to have her doctor write her a prescription, she was thrilled that she'd listened to him.

"It's okay," she told Dan. "I'm safe."

His smile shot through her like a bolt of electricity, setting all her nerve endings on edge. By the time he'd undone her zipper and shoved her jeans down, she was quivering in anticipation. Her skin was damp, almost painfully tender as his fingers glided through the golden curls of hair.

Her entire body clenched at his sweet invasion. She gasped as her hips clenched and writhed, wanting, wanting. "Dan—" She groped for his jeans, but her hands were shaking too much. "Dan . . ."

He drew back only long enough to shed what remained of his clothing and to slide her jeans and panties the rest of the way down her legs and off. Then he brought his hand back to her, stroking deep, sending her higher and higher with each skillful caress. She wasn't anywhere near as dexterous as he was, but he seemed extraordinarily responsive as she trailed her hands across his lightly haired thighs, as she wrapped her fingers around him and fondled every hard, swollen inch of him until he shuddered and nudged her hands away.

Easing her onto her back, he lowered himself into her arms. She opened to him, thoughts of carefree summer fun overtaken by something much more imperative, a mixture of profound need and desperation, an innate knowledge that if Dan didn't take her at once she would be lost.

Then he *did* take her, and she *was* lost, lost in his possession, in his grace and power. He filled her, surged inside her until there was no longer any emptiness, any confusion, until there was nothing but heat and strength and throbbing sensation, bursting through her in rhythmic pulses of ecstasy.

For an endless moment she drifted into a hazy reverie. Dan's rasping groan, and the weight of him as he collapsed wearily onto her, brought her consciousness back into focus. Opening her eyes, she saw a splendorous night sky above. Her arms cradled Dan, savoring his masculine solidity; her shoulder felt the delicate pressure of his lips as he kissed her. Her back felt the bumpy ground beneath the down-filled sleeping bag.

She was sore all over, and she didn't mind one bit.

Dan kissed her shoulder again, then braced his hands on either side of her head and straightened his arms, lifting himself off her.

She immediately tightened her hold on his waist. "Don't."

He gazed down at her. His face glowed with sheer delight in the fire's amber glow; his smile was utterly devoid of mockery or challenge. His body was still locked inside hers. She wanted him there forever.

"I'm crushing you."

"That must make you happy."

He laughed. His hips vibrated against her, and her body flexed instinctively, every nerve twisting taut once more, expectation burning through her. "Don't leave me," she whispered, unsure of what she was pleading for.

He seemed to know. He rocked slowly, gently, sinuously against her until a new eruption overtook her, wringing her with spasms of exquisite pleasure.

Sinking against the pillowy sleeping bag, she closed her eyes and groaned. No doubt about it—she definitely wanted him inside her forever.

But he was spent, as exhausted as she was. Rolling out of her arms, he settled onto the sleeping bag next to her and gathered her to himself in a cozy hug.

"You were right," she said after a while.

"About your passionate nature?"

About that, too, she acknowledged privately. "About having some clean, healthy fun."

He leaned back slightly so he could see her face. He was grinning. "You realize, of course, that because I'm right you owe me your soul for eternity."

"I don't owe you anything," she retorted, although she joined his laughter.

"You don't, huh?" His hand roamed down her back to the roundness of her bottom. He kneaded the soft skin, pulling her against him just enough to remind her of the shimmering satisfaction he'd given her.

"Well . . . I guess I owe you for the dough-boy. All I gave you was a hot dog. That's hardly an even trade."

"Maybe you could smear berry juice all over me and lick it off," he suggested.

Even after the astonishing intimacy they'd just shared, she blushed at the thought. "Dan!"

"Ah, so you're not such a wild woman, after all," he teased. "Sex outdoors by a camp fire is okay, sex with your chief antagonist on Silver Lake is okay, but sex with blueberries is out of the question."

"We all have our limits," she said, adding inwardly that she'd just discovered hers were nowhere near where she'd thought they were.

"Limits are for testing," he declared, abruptly rolling out of her arms and standing.

She propped herself up to watch him as he strode to the camp fire. Neglected for some time, it had died down, but the low flames and luminous embers cast a golden light across his tall, proud body. He looked like a pagan, imbued with magic, standing naked and virile before the gods of earth, fire and sky. Impossible as it seemed, Rebecca's soul stirred with a fresh wave of yearning.

He picked up the pot with the remaining berries and returned to the sleeping bag. As he knelt down, several fireflies flashed beside him, glimmering and vanishing into the dark like sparks of energy.

"I'm not going to smear those onto you," she warned as he stretched out next to her.

"Scaredy-cat," he taunted. She opened her mouth to protest, and he poked a berry between her teeth. "I have every intention of making love with you again, but I've got to fuel up first. Any objections?"

"No," she said in an unusually throaty voice.

No objections at all.

THIS WAS SCARY.

He gazed up at the sloping roof of her tent, which was vaguely lit by the moonlight that sifted inside through the screened flaps. Hours ago he and Rebecca had thrown on some clothes and carried their dishes down to the brook to rinse off the food so it wouldn't attract foraging animals. Then, guided by Dan's flashlight, they'd returned to her tent, stopping at his only long enough for him to retrieve his sleeping bag. It lay under them right now, bunching a bit down toward their feet. Hers was spread on top of them.

Crickets sang through the night. Although Dan and Rebecca had extinguished the fire, the air still held the pungent aroma of pine smoke. Rebecca's head rested against his shoulder, her hair streaming down his arm.

He wanted her.

It *was* just summer fun, wasn't it? They were going to kiss goodbye at the end of August, and he would go back to Pleasant Valley and she would go back to Manhattan and the Claremont School and her upper-crust life. That was what this was about, wasn't it? That was what Dan wanted.

He was too young to make commitments. Much as he looked forward to having the kind of permanent, mature relationship Chuck DeVore enjoyed with Irene, Dan wasn't ready for that yet. All he wanted was...

Rebecca. Again and again and again.

She shifted in the curve of his arm, issuing a low, sultry moan in her sleep. The mere sound of it caused his heart—and other parts of his anatomy—to lurch with desire. His body awakened fully, growing hard, needing her around him once more.

Granted, she was asleep. If one little kiss didn't rouse her, he'd leave it at that.

But one little kiss led to another, bigger one, and in less than a minute her mouth was moving with his, her tongue teasing his, her eyes fluttering open and then closing as she rose onto him. Her skin was warm and velvety against his palms, her breasts lush against his chest, her bottom irresistibly sexy as he massaged the soft flesh, as he rubbed her against his hardness, as he slid himself into the moist heat of her and felt her clench around him in welcome.

Fun, he thought, *this is supposed to be fun.* And it was.

But it was so much more.

She gasped, groaned, ground her hips in a bewitching rhythm. She fisted her hands in his hair and kissed him and shuddered as he thrust deeper and deeper, greedy for all of her, not just her body but her heart, her mind, everything fusing into one magnificent unity. His movements grew more forceful, more aggressive, demanding more and more...and then she went stiff in his arms, balanced on the peak of sensation. He held his breath, then sighed with satisfaction as she succumbed in a fierce cascade of tremors, her body clutching and releasing, pulsing around him, driving him toward his own explosive peak. He was on fire, beyond thought, delirious with the keenest pleasure he'd ever known—and it went on and on, blazing through him until he was no longer sure whether he was still alive, whether one could be alive and in heaven at the same time.

If he were Adam Kember, he would call this awesome. He was Dan Macklin, however, and he called it perfection. Ecstasy. Nirvana.

Rebecca.

"I'm sorry," he whispered, stroking her hair back from her face. Her cheeks were damp, whether from tears or perspiration he didn't know.

"Sorry?"

"For waking you up."

"Oh." With a drowsy laugh she sank down onto him like a blanket, molding her lithe body to his. "I forgive you."

"You're all heart."

"Mmm." She nestled her head into the curve of his shoulder, growing limp and heavy as sleep stole over her once more.

He wrapped his arms around her, willing to let her spend the rest of the night on top of him. His comfort wasn't as important as having her body draped over his, one of her beautiful legs wedged between his thighs, her arm slung across his ribs and strands of her hair snagging in the stubble covering his jaw.

He held her, shut his eyes and inhaled her sensuous female fragrance. Tomorrow, he thought, everything would make sense. He would celebrate this delightful interlude, make plans with her for another night of erotic carousing in the very near future and hike down the hill, following the trail back to Camp Mohawk. Tomorrow he would understand what this was all about.

But tonight he would cling to her and find himself imagining what it would be like to have her every day, every night in his arms, in his thoughts, inhabiting his soul, in sickness and in health, as long as they both shall live. Tonight he would make himself crazy with weird, dangerous fantasies.

HE WOKE UP to an empty tent, the walls and roof blinding orange as the sun beat down. Squinting against the glare, he groped through the pile of his clothing for his watch and held it in front of his face: a quarter to nine.

Outside the tent he heard footsteps and the snap of wood breaking. He threw off Rebecca's sleeping bag, sat up and rubbed the stiff muscles in his lower back. Too much exercise, he thought, shifting his attention to his cramped thigh muscles. A five-mile uphill hike followed by an excessively energetic night with Rebecca had left him aching in all sorts of ways.

Peeking through the mesh of the flap's screen, he saw her moving spryly around the pit, constructing a pyre of firewood. He hastened to get dressed, tucked his toothbrush into a pocket and carried his boots outside to put on.

Her hands full of kindling, Rebecca turned to greet him. The unadorned affection in her smile hit him like a fist to his stomach. She was too beautiful, too lovely. Just looking at her as the bright morning sun turned her hair to platinum and her cheeks to rose made him insane with desire.

"Good morning," she said.

Her simple greeting provoked too many complicated emotions inside him. He wanted to haul her into his arms and kiss her; he wanted to bury his lips against her throat and recite passages of French poetry, or even obscene jokes about mermaids. He wanted to take his tongue—his tongue of love—and run it over every square inch of her body.

Exercising restraint, he returned her smile and said, "Good morning."

Lacing his boots, he watched as she arranged the sticks in the center of the pit, then broke a thicker stick over her knee and began a log-cabin construction around the kindling. He hurriedly finished with his boots, anxious to give her a hand.

Then he hesitated. Yesterday she had thanked him for letting her take care of herself. She might resent his assistance in building the fire.

What was wrong with him? Why was he hovering near the tent, fidgeting with his boot laces and tormenting himself over whether or not he should help her? What had she done to make him so hypersensitive? They'd had sex, and it was great, but that didn't mean he had to analyze his every impulse and predict her reactions, did it?

"My canteen's empty," she called over her shoulder. "If you're going down to the brook, would you mind filling it up for me?"

"No problem." He lifted it along with his own and headed across the field to the stream, grateful for the opportunity to get away from her and clear his head.

Alone in the shadows, he washed up, filled the canteens and wrestled with his thoughts. It bothered him that she was so chipper and vigorous when he was painfully conscious of every tired muscle in his body. It bothered him even more that, other than her uncommonly good mood, she didn't seem the least bit affected by last night.

Well, a good mood was something, he supposed. The smile she'd given him when he emerged from the tent told him she'd had no second thoughts about what they'd done, no misgivings, no regrets.

He had no second thoughts, misgivings or regrets, either. Yet he felt uneasy, unsettled, as if he'd somehow trespassed onto alien terrain. He'd hoped he would come to his senses in the morning, but the moment he'd seen her he had felt overcome with romantic fancies.

This was definitely scary.

He was subdued as he returned to the campfire, lugging the full canteens. Rebecca's breakfast supplies consisted of an assortment of powders: powdered eggs, powdered coffee, powdered milk. He offered to share his rolled oats with her, and she gleefully returned her powdered eggs to her backpack. "We can toss some blueberries in," she suggested as he filled a pot with water and set it on the fire.

Memories of his previous night's X-rated blueberry-juice fantasies visited him, sending a shiver down his spine. Even in her shorts and T-shirt, her thick socks and bulky hiking shoes, she was unbearably sexy. When he'd told Chuck she was his obsession, he hadn't realized how dangerously obsessed he could become.

She tucked a stray lock of hair behind her ear. His abdomen tensed. Even her earlobes were enchanting.

"Uh, Rebecca . . ." He cleared his throat. He didn't know what he should say, but he had to say something. Something about love, maybe. Something about how she was infinitely more exciting than he'd ever dared to expect, and he was sorry he'd given her such a hard time during her first few weeks at Silver

Lake, and he hoped they could be friends for a long time. Something like that.

She stirred the oatmeal, then raised her beautiful gray eyes to him. "Yes?"

"Um . . ." He took a deep breath. "Last night was great."

She gave him another dazzling smile. "It was. I guess you're not such a creep, after all."

He smiled tentatively. What she'd said was a compliment, but it didn't exactly bowl him over.

Why the hell should he *want* to be bowled over? This was a treacherous situation. One wrong move, and he could be baring his soul and pledging his troth.

His smile expanded. "No," he agreed, deciding her lighthearted attitude was a lot safer than his emotional approach. "I can be extraordinarily uncreepy when the planets are in the proper configuration."

"And when you aren't pulling one of your practical jokes." She lifted the oatmeal pot from the fire and spooned some cereal into his plate. "I like you, Dan."

He eyed her cautiously. What did she mean by that? Did she like him, or did she *like* him? Should he return the tribute or run for cover?

Before he could decide how to respond, she continued. "I know we've had our run-ins, but last night was . . . I don't think 'great' begins to describe it."

He smiled and waited for her to go on.

"I'd like to think we can trust each other."

"Of course." What was she getting at? More sex? Less fun? Were they going to have to behave like grown-ups now?

She twirled her spoon thoughtfully through her oatmeal. "I've never done anything like this before."

"Anything like what?"

Her cheeks took on a rosy hue again, and he knew it wasn't from the sun. "That stuff I said yesterday about my passionate nature—well, I wasn't just saying that. It's usually true."

He detected a definite trend away from light-hearted toward emotional. He decided to go along with it for now and see where it led. "I think you're very passionate," he told her.

"Something special happened last night," she said, gazing directly at him. "And I'm not sorry."

"Neither am I."

"Well," she said briskly, "I've got to hit the trail right after breakfast. I'm supposed to be back at Chippewa by noon."

Don't run off! he almost shouted. *Let's make love one more time!* "They won't shoot you if you get there a few minutes late."

"No, but the middle girls are having their summer art exposition this afternoon. I'm supposed to hand out blue ribbons for the best artworks—which means I've got to think of fifty different categories so everyone can win. I've got to see to some final details for our trip to see *Peter Pan,* too."

"A camp director's job is never done," Dan confirmed in a dry voice.

"I'm really looking forward to the trip," she went on between spoonfuls of oatmeal and sips of instant coffee. "The girls have already learned most of the songs from the show. My favorite is 'Tender Shepherd.' It's such a pretty lullaby.''

"Mine is 'I Won't Grow Up.'"

"Why doesn't that surprise me?" Rebecca said with a laugh.

He opened his mouth to argue, then shut it. What could he say in his own defense? That he hadn't wanted to grow up until last night? That he was willing to grow up if it meant she would be willing to...to what? What did he actually want from her?

He scrutinized her as she turned from the fire and began to dismantle her tent. The orange nylon collapsed, one end at a time, as she untied the stays. He found the sight depressing.

What if he made some sort of proclamation, a promise, a profession of love—and she laughed at him?

What if he made a promise and she took him up on it?

Why couldn't he simply say "Thanks for the fun, let's do it again soon"?

Why did being a manly man seem so much less important than being a man?

Chapter Eleven

The drizzle saturating the air matched Rebecca's mood perfectly. She lingered on the porch of the administration building Friday evening as the senior girls lined the path to the recreation hall, every third one armed with an umbrella to form a makeshift canopy for the visiting Mohawks. Trooping off the bus in yellow slickers and green ponchos, the boys shouted boisterous salutations to the girls. After several weekly socials, they'd gotten to know each other pretty well.

The last one off the bus was Dan.

Rebecca remained on the porch, staring at him through the gloomy mist, pretending that the mere sight of him didn't send her nervous system into an uproar. She wanted to feel nothing when she saw him, nothing at all.

He hadn't spoken to her since they'd parted ways at the blueberry patch two and a half days ago. He hadn't phoned, hadn't driven over, hadn't canoed across the lake. Taking the initiative, she had telephoned him Thursday afternoon and had been told that he was somewhere in the woods on a cook-out with a junior-boys bunk. She'd left her name with the clerk, but Dan hadn't bothered to return her call.

So this was what he meant by clean, healthy summer fun, she fumed, disgusted with him for being such a juvenile jerk and with herself for having responded to him so profoundly that one night. So this was what was meant by simplifying things: wham-bam, thank you ma'am.

Lord help her, she'd actually thought that through their lovemaking she and Dan had reached some sort of understanding. She had developed powerful insights into herself—discovering not just what he called her passionate nature, but her capacity for cutting loose, letting go, doing something audacious not as a rebellion or a crusade but simply because the time, the place, the mood and the man were right.

As for her passionate nature, well, that had certainly been an astounding discovery. Nothing in her life had prepared her for the things Dan had made her feel, made her want. She'd known the facts of life before that night, but not the *truth*—not until he'd opened her eyes and her heart to it.

The following morning she'd been tempted to hurl herself at him, to beg him to stay on the hilltop with her forever, disregarding their obligations, cutting themselves off from the real world and subsisting on blueberries and love. She'd longed to throw her arms around him and call him her lover. She'd never had a lover before. She'd never met a man for whom the word seemed appropriate.

Until Dan.

The dolt. The jerk. The idiotic Hawk hunk who could spend all of a divine night romancing her and then saunter down a trail and out of her life without even a farewell wave.

He must have spotted her, because he halted on the path and shielded his eyes to survey the administration building. He had on a khaki-colored rain jacket, a green Camp Mohawk shirt and jeans. Rebecca was wearing jeans, too. She hadn't felt like getting fixed up nicely on such a damp, dreary evening. Apparently neither had he.

He veered off the path, strolling in her direction, and she reluctantly descended from the porch. Through the recreation hall screen doors she could hear the social gearing up, and she knew she ought to be with the campers. But this awkward reunion with Dan was something she'd have to go through sooner or later. She might as well get it over with now.

"Hi," he said, offering a surprisingly shy smile. His eyes reminded her of the ocean at night, green, blue, filled with life and shadows.

She wished a thousand curses upon his head for being so insufferably good-looking. "Hi," she said.

"How are you?"

Small talk? After the most feverish, glorious, rapturous lovemaking the world had ever seen, was this what they were reduced to? "Oh, just fine," she answered airily, casting a longing look toward the recreation hall.

"Any chance you'll save a dance for me?"

She turned back and presented him with a sweet, ingratiating smile. "I'd rather eat razor blades," she said, then pivoted and walked in dignified strides down the path to the hall.

Once inside, she found it relatively easy to steer clear of him. She stationed herself here and there, studying the dancing, chattering boys and girls.

Some fervent alliances had formed between individual Hawks and Chippies, she noticed. Especially the lovebirds of the century, Stephanie Glynn and Adam Kember. Tonight she was wearing his leather necklace. Did that mean they were going steady, or that he wanted to put her on a leash?

Rebecca stifled her cynicism. Just because she had come to believe that romance was a vastly overrated phenomenon didn't mean no one could indulge in it.

Occasionally she caught a glimpse of Dan through the crowd. Whenever their eyes met, she sent him one of her falsely placid smiles. Regardless of what had happened several days ago, they were rational, mature camp directors now, chaperoning their campers and making sure no one got into trouble.

Maggie Tyrell waved to her from the refreshment table. "Soda's running low," she shouted. "You want me to bring over some more bottles?"

"I'll do it," Rebecca shouted back. She grabbed one of the umbrellas propped up near the door, stepped outside and picked her way among the puddles to the dining hall.

Entering the kitchen, she heard her footsteps echoing behind her. She snapped shut the umbrella, took a few steps farther into the brightly lit room and heard the sound again. It wasn't an echo. Someone was following her, pursuing her through the dining room.

Brandishing the umbrella in front of her like a lance, she spun toward the kitchen door and came face-to-face with Dan Macklin.

They sized each other up in silence. His hair was limp, and his cheeks and brow glistened with raindrops. She contrasted his clean-shaven jaw with the stubble he'd had the last time she'd seen him, and experienced an unwanted memory of the way his chin had chafed her cheeks and breasts, the scratchy sound it had made against her fingernails. She squeezed the handle of the umbrella as tightly as she could and prayed for the memory to pass.

He smiled and crossed the threshold.

"Thanks, anyway," she said crisply, "but I don't need any help."

"Becky." Still smiling, he shook his head and took another step toward her, his arms outstretched.

She raised the umbrella higher, pointing its tip at his throat. When he fell back, she sighed, set her weapon down on the stainless-steel table beside her and turned away. Much as she'd love to gore him with the umbrella, she couldn't. Not that she had any qualms about committing acts of violence on him, but she didn't want him to know how much his refusal to see her or talk to her had hurt. A failure to live up to promises he'd never even made wasn't exactly grounds for homicide.

"Rebecca, don't be angry. I wanted to call you," he said, his voice low and husky, sounding much too intimate given their surroundings.

"I'm sure you've been busy," she said, stalking to one of the walk-in refrigerators. "No harm done, Dan. I know how it is."

"You *don't* know how it is." He had crossed the room to stand behind her. She could feel his warmth, sense it along her spine, against the nape of her neck, in her shoulders an instant before his hands alighted on them. He turned her around and smiled down at her. "Give me a kiss, Rebecca."

"Are you crazy? Why should I give you a kiss?"

"Why?" He brushed his lips lightly over hers, flooding her with sensations, with more unwanted memories of the way he'd felt on top of her, underneath her, inside her. Her sharp gasp resounded against the hard steel and tile surfaces of the room. "That's why," he murmured, brushing his lips over hers again, gently coaxing.

She wriggled out of his embrace and slipped away from the refrigerator. "Don't."

"I thought you said you liked me."

His accusation sounded absurdly callow, the sort of thing a child might shout at a traitorous playmate in the school yard. "Oh, I like you just fine, Dan," she declared, pleased that her voice had lost its desperate edge. "I think you're swell. I just don't want to kiss you."

"Listen, Rebecca..." He ran his fingers through his thick damp hair, shoving it back from his face in frustration. "I don't know what's going on anymore. This whole thing between us has been bizarre. I'm not used to it. Give me a break."

"I'd be delighted. Would you rather I break your arm or your leg?"

He grinned, although his gaze remained solemn. "I'm serious, okay? I'm sorry I didn't return your call—"

"Forget it." She waved off his apology with a flutter of her hand.

"I won't forget it. It's not like I didn't want to talk to you. It's just..." He sighed again. "I'm really confused."

"Don't worry about it. Confusion is curable. I used to be confused, but now I'm completely over it."

He held up his hands in surrender. "All right, I confess. I'm guilty. I should have called. I should have come to see you. I should have taken you out for dinner at a restaurant with a wine list your father would approve of. I'm sorry, Rebecca, but I'm still trying to learn my way around this thing."

"What thing?"

He raked his hand through his hair again, then shook his head. "Taking the long view. Thinking about the future." He paused. "Growing up."

She eyed him curiously. "Are you growing up?"

He shrugged and risked taking a step closer to her.

She was too intrigued to object to his nearness. "On my account?" she asked.

"I don't know. Like I said, I'm pretty damned confused at the moment."

She leaned against the refrigerator door, folded her arms and appraised him thoughtfully. She was fascinated by the prospect of Dan Macklin being pretty damned confused. She ought to have been alienated—his cocky self-confidence was part of his attraction. Yet he seemed just as attractive to her now, with the front of his shirt damp enough to reveal the contours of his chest, and water streaking in rivulets down his cheeks.

"Go ahead, say it," he goaded her. "I'm the one sending mixed signals now."

She gazed up into his solemn eyes. "You are."

"You're so beautiful, Becky."

Nothing mixed in that signal. She decided to preempt him before his flattery led her astray. As it was, she was getting pretty damned confused herself. "Please don't kiss me, Dan."

"Okay." He plunged his hands into his pockets and mirrored her steady gaze. "How about talking? Can we do that?"

"Not now. In case you forgot, we've got a bunch of campers going at it in the rec hall."

He nodded. "How about tomorrow? Will you have any free time?"

"The whole camp is going to see *Peter Pan*," she said. "We'll be gone all day. Maybe in the evening, if you'd like to call me." No way would she call him again. Let him make the next move, the next several moves. Let him prove that he truly intended to take the long view and grow up. Let her have a chance to assess this new, serious side of Dan Macklin and decide what she thought about it.

Loath though she was to admit it, she suspected she would like the new Dan a lot. As long as he still laughed sometimes, as long as he still favored doughboys over hot dogs, as long as he didn't divest himself of all his appealing boyishness. As long as he didn't turn into a Wallace clone and turn his back on the magic they had shared in the blueberry patch a few nights ago.

"Tomorrow evening, then," he promised, extending his arm to her. Cautiously she slipped her hand into his. He pulled her toward him, but instead of trying to kiss her he only enveloped her in a gentle hug. His arms felt good around her, his body solid and strong. Holding him reminded her of the night they'd spent together, the wicked, wonderful things he'd made her feel.

So, he wanted to talk. Resting her head against his shoulder, inhaling his familiar scent and reveling in his powerful embrace, she acknowledged how very much she wanted to listen.

THE TRIP WAS a huge success. Rebecca rode home in the bus with the middle campers, whose favorite song from the show was clearly, "I've Got a Crow." For the entire half-hour ride back to the camp, they squawked and screamed and cackled and clucked.

Seated next to one of the counselors at the front of the bus, Rebecca accepted the cacophony with a tolerant smile. For the most part she had tried to perform her camp-director duties as she believed Chuck would have done them, but she prided herself on adding a few innovations to Camp Chippewa's routine. That evening she would have to call Artie Birnbaum and inform him of what a triumph the theater trip had been.

That evening she would talk to Dan, too. Her smile grew meditative as she tried to guess what they would talk about. Had he truly undergone some significant change in his needs and aspirations? Was she responsible for the change?

Should she dare to imagine that Dan would still want to be in her life once August gave way to September? Should she dare to imagine that she would want the same thing?

Intellectually she swore to herself that all she wanted was a summer fling with him. But in her heart, in her soul…lord help her, but she wanted *him*. She wanted his brilliant eyes and his mischievous mind, his glorious body and his whimsical approach to life. She wanted to take the long view with him.

"We're starving to death," the camper in the seat behind her shouted. "Are we going to have dinner as soon as we get back to camp?"

Rebecca checked her watch: nearly six. "Yes. Do you think you'll survive till then?"

"I don't know," the girl said, clutching her throat and making dire gagging noises. The camper next to her joined in, lolling her tongue and rolling her eyes.

"Too much drama in these kids' lives," the counselor whispered to Rebecca. "Now they all want to be actresses."

"As long as they don't want to be Wendy," Rebecca whispered back. "The way Wendy doted on all those lost boys so they would never have to grow up…"

"That's a universal girlhood fantasy," the counselor pointed out.

"Fortunately most of us outgrow it."

The counselor grinned knowingly and nodded.

The three buses reached the final approach to Camp Chippewa, and the girls spilled from the buses for the dining room. Rebecca was signing the check for the bus rentals when the first screams filtered through the pine trees. She sprinted to the heart of the camp, trying not to let the increasing volume of hysterical shrieks and laughter alarm her.

Then she saw for herself what the tumult was about: a continuous clothesline had been strung from cabin to cabin to cabin. Hanging from the clothesline were shoes.

Girls' shoes. Hundreds of them. Her campers' shoes.

"Oh, my God," she gasped, nudging aside a few strident Chippies and inspecting a clothesline. Sneakers and moccasins; rubber flip-flops and leather sandals; a Minnie Mouse beach shoe and a leather wedgie all dangled from the rope in a mismatched jumble. The only common element was that they were all for the left foot.

"Oh, my God," she reiterated, this time in a quiet wail.

Maggie Tyrell elbowed a path to her side through the throngs of campers. "He did this throughout the camp."

Rebecca didn't have to ask who "he" was. She pursed her lips and surveyed the clotheslines. "It's going to take forever to straighten this out," she muttered.

A camper came over, a pink flip-flop in one hand and a blue one in the other. "We're gonna get them back, huh, Rebecca," she swore. "We really gonna have to get those dumb Hawks back, but good."

"Sure," Rebecca agreed. But her heart wasn't in it. Pressing her fingertips to her temples to ward off an encroaching headache, she turned and stalked away from the fracas.

She wished she could think about some suitable revenge. But all she could think of was a group of over-aged boys singing "I won't grow up!"—under the baton of their very own Peter Pan.

AT LEAST THIS TIME she'd had the guts to take his call, he thought, climbing into a canoe and drifting toward the center of the lake. At least this time she hadn't had that secretary of hers running interference.

Then again, talking to Rebecca that evening hadn't been the most enjoyable experience of his life. She'd had to leave a campwide shoe-sorting session to take his call. Before he could even get a hello out, she'd lit into him: "What on earth is wrong with you? Do you realize it's seven-thirty and we're still trying to find people's shoes?"

"Rebecca—"

"I hope you're happy, Dan. I hope you're really proud of yourself. This stupid, childish mischief spoiled everyone's day."

What was he supposed to say? "Sure, sweetheart—and when you're all done with the shoes, can I come over and have sex with you?"

He tried for contrition instead. "Becky, I'm sorry. It wasn't exactly my idea—"

"You mean, there's more than one pervert running the show at Camp Mohawk?"

Pervert? Where the hell was her sense of humor? "What's the big deal? The Hawks wanted to have a little fun. Don't take this stuff so seriously, Rebecca. It was just a joke."

"You're right," she snapped. "I shouldn't take it seriously. When it comes to you, Dan, I shouldn't take anything seriously. And now, if you'll excuse me, I've got to go. There's a little girl outside my door sobbing because her bunny-rabbit slipper is missing. Obviously *she's* taking it much too seriously."

A click, and the line was dead.

He drifted into the center of the lake, cutting his paddle through the still surface of the water with a minimum of splash. Above him the moon was on the wane, dim enough not to detract from the glittering magnificence of the stars. Dan turned the canoe to face north, where the shoreline rose in a steep incline. He thought about the bluff, about the blueberries, about Rebecca.

How had everything gotten so complicated? How had she gotten him so twisted up? Summers past, this shoe gag would have been hailed as an achievement of the highest order. Chuck would have toasted Dan with a beer.

Of course, Chuck wasn't a beautiful blond woman with a body that could perform wonders, that could awaken every cell in Dan to the sublime pleasures of passion. Chuck wasn't Rebecca.

Why her? Why, of all people, did he have to get hung up on her? Was it because she was convenient? Chuck himself had reminded Dan that there were plenty of other women summering in the Catskills, if Dan cared to look.

He didn't care to. He wanted only Rebecca. As recently as last night, he'd been contemplating the very real possibility that he was in love with her.

How could he be in love with someone who didn't have a sense of humor? How could he be in love with such an arrogant twit?

He couldn't. He simply couldn't.

Without realizing it, he had let the canoe float toward the western shore, the pebbly stretch of coastline from which a path led to Rebecca's cabin. He adamantly paddled the canoe around to face east, and propelled the craft in strong, sure strokes to his own shore.

The hell with her. The hell with love. If she couldn't laugh, he didn't want her.

Chapter Twelve

Hearing the knock on her cabin door, Rebecca instantly thought of peacock feathers.

The feather bouquet Dan had brought her several weeks ago was currently stashed in the bottom drawer of her rustic maple dresser. She hadn't been able to throw it out, but she couldn't stand looking at it, either. It was very much the way she felt about Dan himself—she didn't want to see him, yet she couldn't bear the thought of never seeing him again.

So far, never seeing him again had lasted five days. She had spoken to him only once, when he subjected her to a five-minute tirade about what a grumpy, cranky prig she was. He'd concluded by thanking her for divesting him of his confusion. "I'm not the least bit confused about you anymore, Pruitt," he'd declared. "Thanks for straightening me out."

She was willing to admit—to herself if no one else— that maybe she had overreacted to the shoe business. But if she had, the fault lay with Dan. He had told her he wanted to grow up, and she'd foolishly believed he meant it. She had no desire to play the role of Wendy, indulging the silly antics of a man-sized boy.

On the other hand, she didn't want to be a little wifey to a solid, stolid businessman like Wallace.

Her father had called her, just minutes after Dan's call, to tell her he had spotted Wallace squiring Gwen Veebeck around town. "Well, here's the news I want to get back to him," she'd countered. "I wish him and Gwen the very best."

It was true. She'd felt genuine relief to know that Wallace was seeing another woman. Rebecca had never wanted anything but happiness for him, and she knew she wasn't the woman to make him happy.

She wanted happiness for herself, too—the timeless, boundless happiness she'd known with Dan that one fateful night. But apparently Dan couldn't be depended on to make her happy.

She heard another, louder knock at her door. If he had the gall to come sneaking up on her with some cutesy peace offering again, she thought as she went to answer it, she'd slam the door on him.

Maggie Tyrell stood on the step, carrying a flashlight and looking worried. "We've got a problem," she announced.

Rebecca considered the odds that Dan had set Maggie up, that this was part of some elaborate new hoax. But from the look on Maggie's face, she discounted that possibility. "What is it?"

"Put on your hiking shoes and grab a flashlight," Maggie urged her. "This is a biggie."

Curiosity blended with skepticism. "Have the ninnies from Mohawk pulled another intercamp stunt?" Rebecca asked as she wiggled her feet into her boots.

"One ninny has," Maggie confirmed. "Come on, hurry. You'll hear everything when we get to the office."

Taking a deep breath, Rebecca grabbed her flashlight and followed her assistant out of the cabin. If Dan Macklin was the ninny behind this late-evening summons, she would find out soon enough.

When they reached the office, Maggie stepped inside, gesturing for Rebecca to precede her. For a brief, paranoid moment she wondered if something would fall on her when she opened the door—maybe a bucket of water or a cream pie.

Squaring her shoulders, gritting her teeth and preparing to hate Dan to her dying day, she turned the knob and shoved open the door.

He stood directly across from the door, looking as solemn as Maggie. He was dressed for night hiking, with a flashlight and an unfolded map in his hand. Next to him stood one of his counselors and one of hers.

"What's going on?" she asked, swallowing the nervous quiver in her voice.

"Adam Kember and one of your girls ran away," Dan announced.

"What?"

"Stephanie Glynn," the Chippewa counselor said, her voice cracking. "Oh, God, Rebecca, I'm so sorry! I don't know how she could have gotten away. I just—"

"Shh." Rebecca held up her hand to silence the counselor, then turned back to Dan. "Two of our campers ran away? Together?"

"Sometime after lights-out at Mohawk, Adam snuck out of his bunk, stole a canoe and paddled across the lake—"

"And no one at Mohawk caught him?" Rebecca exclaimed. "What kind of supervision have you got there?"

"Hey, it happened, okay?" Dan eyed her coolly, steadily, as if awaiting another outburst. When Rebecca held her tongue, he continued. "Adam got to Chippewa, went to Stephanie's bunk—"

"I'm so sorry," Stephanie's counselor began to babble again. "I had just gone into the staff house to get a can of soda, and when I came back to check the cabin, she was gone. It's all my fault, Rebecca, I swear—"

"It's not your fault." Rebecca sounded far calmer than she felt. She had lost a camper! A camper had vanished into the woods, into the night, with a boy! Good God, something terrible could happen to them—and if anyone was ultimately accountable, it was Rebecca.

And Dan. His damned camper had started the whole thing. Adam Kember had no doubt been following the example of his impulsive, immature leader. Who cared about rules and responsibilities when you could have fun?

There would be time to assign blame later. Right now Rebecca had to find Stephanie, and fast.

"What time frame are we talking about?" she asked. "When did they leave?"

"Maybe a half hour ago," the counselor estimated. "Maybe less. I'm not exactly sure."

"They couldn't have gotten that far, then."

"Not unless they headed for the road and hitched a ride," Maggie noted.

The possibility slammed into Rebecca with shocking force, and she bit her lip to keep from screaming. What if Stephanie and Adam had hitchhiked? What if— She couldn't consider it. She couldn't let herself succumb to pessimism or panic. "I think we ought to notify the police."

Maggie darted around the counter to the phone and began dialing the number of the Silver Lake Police Department.

"Meanwhile," Dan resolved, "let's organize a search. Pete, you and Cindy can take this route south, and Rebecca and I can head north—" he traced the routes on the map "—and meanwhile, Maggie can stay here and work with the police. I brought some walkie-talkies over from Mohawk so we can all keep in contact with each other."

"Okay," Rebecca agreed. Ordinarily she would resent having to defer to him, but he appeared much less rattled than she felt. Maybe his unruffled demeanor was a pretense, as hers was. But his attitude didn't seem fake. He seemed more levelheaded than she'd ever seen him before.

She huddled with him and the counselors, scrutinizing the map. "Have you got a photocopy machine?" he asked. "We could make a copy of this."

"Sure. It's in the corner over there," she said, pointing out the machine against the back wall. "I'll get some Coleman lanterns. They give off a lot more light than the flashlights."

"Good idea," said Dan, lifting the map and moving around the counter in long, efficient strides.

Rebecca raced to the supply shed to get the lamps. She tuned out the dark tranquility of Camp Chippewa at night. She ignored, as well, the frisson of pleasure Dan's offhanded praise had given her. Of course the lanterns were a good idea. Just because she was upset didn't mean she'd forgotten how to think.

Dan and the counselors were on the porch waiting for her when she returned with two bulky lamps. Dan lit one, then handed it to Cindy and lit the other. Rebecca noticed the rectangular black walkie-talkie hanging on his belt next to his flashlight, above his left hip. A canteen hung on a strap over his right shoulder.

"Stick together and stay on the trails and the road," he instructed the counselors in a low, intense voice. "We'll meet back here in forty-five minutes, unless we find them sooner."

"Right."

"Good luck."

They all nodded gravely. Then Cindy and Pete started south, the Coleman lamp spreading a bright white glow ahead of them.

Dan exchanged a cryptic look with Rebecca, then turned and started north. She shoved her hands into the pockets of her jeans and fell into step beside him. They walked silently past the cabins and found the first markers of the trail that led around the lake, up to the bluff.

Ordinarily Rebecca would have endured a night-time hike with equanimity. Tonight, however, the looming shadows and silhouettes of the fir trees closed in on her, making her think of specters and ghouls. She heard the faint scratching noises of scurrying animals; she felt their eyes upon her. The hooting of an owl sent a chill down her spine.

Oh, God, she was scared.

"What?" Dan asked.

She glanced at Dan, startled. Had she spoken aloud without realizing it, or had he read her mind?

"You keep twitching your shoulders. Are you cold?"

"No." Her voice sounded mournful. "I'm just…a little worried."

"That's understandable."

She had expected mocking, not sympathy. "Are you worried?"

He shrugged. "I think we'll come out of this okay."

She had to remind herself that he was referring to their search for the campers and nothing more. If they came out of their search okay—with Adam and Stephanie safe and sound and in their custody—Rebecca promised herself she would be satisfied.

Still, seeing Dan after so many days of anger and indignation disconcerted her. When she thought of him taking charge, she thought of him leading his band of Hawks in zany, irritating shenanigans, not organizing a rescue mission. To see him behaving so composed and authoritative and...well, mature... She didn't know what to think.

Except that she was enormously grateful. In spite of everything, she knew she could depend on him tonight, and she was glad of it.

"I can't believe something like this could happen on my watch," she murmured, once again aware of the grief in her voice. "I feel so responsible—"

"These things happen," he said, arching his arm around her shoulders, giving her an affectionate hug and then releasing her. "We're running summer camps, not prison camps. We can't exactly chain the kids to their bunk beds at night."

"Maybe we should."

The path grew narrower, more overgrown. Their footsteps crunched and rustled against the foliage. Dan held the lantern high enough to illuminate not just the trail but the brush and trees on either side. A flutter of wings to their left as an owl swooped from a high branch caused him to stop and scan the forest.

"Adam!" he hollered into the darkness. "Stephanie!"

Rebecca cupped her hands around her mouth and shouted into the darkness.

They waited. No response. They resumed their hike.

Rebecca felt her shoulders twitch again. "What if they did hitch a ride?"

"Then the police will take over." He gave her another consoling hug. "Don't worry about it. Let's just hope for the best, okay?"

"I wish I could. But I keep thinking of all the horrible things that could happen to them, and it's my fault. I'm the director. I'm accountable."

"Stephanie's accountable. Adam, too. They've got to take responsibility for what they've done."

"How can you be so calm?"

His smile was mirthless. "What other choice is there?" He patted her arm and lifted the lantern higher. "Let's keep calling for them."

They shouted the campers' names into the darkness. The only response they heard was the caw of a crow.

They continued on the trail. Dan held a branch back for Rebecca; she held one back for him. The night air was astringent, crisp and dry and fragrant. Dan's presence steadied her.

"Am I going too fast?" he asked after a couple of minutes passed in silence.

"No."

"Warm enough?"

"I'm fine," she said—an overstatement, but at least physically she was all right. His brisk gait suited her. If she was shivering, it wasn't because she was cold.

The path grew more rugged, twisting, climbing, bulging with roots and stones. Rebecca's toe caught on a protruding root, and she lost her balance. Dan grabbed her arm and held her upright.

Her heart pounded furiously, not from her near fall, not from Dan's clasp but from sheer, unadulterated terror.

Evidently Dan felt her trembling. He pulled her against him and held her, allowing her to absorb his strength, his confidence. "It's okay to be afraid, you know," he murmured into her hair.

"You're not afraid."

"Let's just say I'm extremely concerned."

"Then why aren't you shaking and whimpering, too?" she asked, lifting her face from his shoulder.

He laughed. "Only one of us can shake and whimper at a time," he explained.

"Do you want a turn? I'll try to be stoical if you want."

"That's all right. Manly men don't shake and whimper, at least not in front of witnesses."

A faint smile teased her lips. She straightened up, and he loosened his embrace.

"Let's shout together," he suggested.

They raised their hands and bellowed, *"Stephanie! Adam!"*

Nothing.

"Why don't you hold the lantern?" He handed it to her. "This stretch of the trail is kind of tricky."

Rebecca took the glowing gas lamp from him. They started walking. The lantern hissed as its gas fuel seeped through the valves. Dan's breathing was deep and even.

In the weeks she'd known him, he had sparked a dizzying assortment of sentiments in her, from torrid desire to searing hatred, from amusement to exasperation to self-protective retreat. But never, as she'd swung from one extreme to the other, had she felt as safe as she did now. Never had she endowed him with such unshakable faith.

He didn't belittle her fear, yet he refused to knuckle under to it. Whatever she needed—a touch, a bracing hug, a brighter light on the path before her—he provided it without question, without hesitation. Where someone else might have sheltered her from this disaster or dumped the entire calamity into her lap, Dan simply shared it with her, two equals facing a difficult and possibly dangerous predicament together. Two colleagues. Two comrades.

Two friends.

"Adam! Stephanie!"

"Over here!" came a faint, high-pitched voice to their right.

Rebecca was so startled she nearly stumbled again. Dan clamped his hand on her shoulder and held her motionless. "Stephanie!" he roared.

From a distance, through the dark, came the sound of twigs snapping, something thumping against the ground, and then a boy's voice, half-changed from alto to tenor, yelling, "Dumb chick!"

"That's Adam," Dan whispered to Rebecca.

She held the lamp high. A weak amber light skittered and bounced through the dark woods, followed by a scuffling noise and Stephanie's whine, "Stupid idiot!"

"We'd better go in before they kill each other," Dan recommended. Rebecca nodded and moved cautiously off the trail and into the woods, gauging each step before she took it.

Traipsing through the deep shadows was arduous, but eventually they made it to a small clearing. Stephanie stood on one side, clinging to the nearly dead flashlight, while Adam sat on the ground as far from her as possible, his back against a tree and a scowl on his face.

"He's such a dork!" Stephanie screeched, flinging herself at Rebecca. "I never want to see his pig face again!"

"Love is a many-splendored thing," Dan muttered wryly.

Over the low drone of Dan's voice on the walkie-talkie as he reported in to Maggie, Stephanie clung to Rebecca and whined. "He's so awful, Rebecca! You know what he did? He ate all the candy bars we brought, every single one! We were supposed to save them for when we got hungry, but he ate them all. He said he loved me. He said he wanted to marry me."

"*Marry* you! You're only fourteen!"

"That's why he said we would go south. They let you get married real young in Maryland, or maybe it was Alabama. I don't know."

"I hate to tell you this, Stephanie, but you were headed north, not south."

"See?" she jeered at Adam. "Shows how much you know, you jerk!"

"I told you," he said with exaggerated patience, "we were gonna hide out in the woods tonight and head south tomorrow."

"Yeah, and meanwhile, you ate all our food. I could've starved to death out here!"

Rebecca tightened her arms around Stephanie, overcome with relief. In time she'd lambaste the kids for running away, but for now she was simply going to celebrate having them back.

Stephanie was hardly in a celebratory mood. "Not only did he eat every last candy bar, but I was freezing, and he wouldn't give me his jacket—"

"I told her to bring her own jacket, but did she? No-o-o-o!"

"I forgot. Shoot me, why don't you?"

"Yeah. That would spare the planet another dumb chick."

"I'm not a chick! I hate that word."

"Okay, okay," Dan interjected, grabbing Adam's wrist and yanking him to his feet. "Why don't we head back to camp and continue the love fest there?"

The hike back took less time than the hike out; the path was mostly downhill. But Stephanie and Adam bickered the entire time. Stephanie accused him of being selfish, egotistical, bossy and unconscionably infantile. Adam accused her of having a big butt. Stephanie burst into tears. "I thought I loved you!" she wailed. "I thought you were the neatest guy in the world. I would have gone anywhere with you. And that's all you can say?"

"It's true," Adam sneered.

By eleven o'clock they reached the administration building, where they were welcomed by Maggie, the two counselors, a police officer and a pot full of fresh-brewed coffee.

Once the campers were returned to their bunks and the policeman's questions answered, Rebecca and Dan sat drinking steaming cups of coffee. "I think we ought to call the kids' parents," Dan said. "I don't know about you, but I may decide to send Adam home."

"Are we allowed to do that? The kids' parents paid for a full summer session."

Dan rubbed a weary hand along his chin. "Mohawk's contract contains a clause about behavior that imperils the safe functioning of the camp. I don't know if this qualifies, but it's a possibility."

"I guess I'll discuss it with Artie Birnbaum," Rebecca responded. "There may be some insurance considerations."

Dan nodded. "Last week Adam asked his counselor to buy him contraceptives. The kid's really pushing the limits, you know?"

"Contraceptives?" Rebecca felt a fresh stab of horror. What if they'd come across Stephanie and Adam in the act? "That little rat!"

"What?"

"Telling her he wanted to marry her, and then he lured her into the woods with the intention of having his way with her."

Dan eyed her dubiously. "Now, just a second here. Your little Chippie wasn't exactly blameless."

"She thought they were getting married! I mean, isn't that just like a man? Promise her anything—"

"He isn't a man, Rebecca. He's fourteen."

"And he's already got the moves down pat. It turns my stomach. I can just picture him ten years from now, conning unsuspecting women out of their inheritances. And twenty years from now, running for political office. Send him home, Dan. I don't want him within a hundred miles of my girls."

Dan appeared to be wrestling with a laugh. "You take care of your camper, and I'll take care of mine."

She let out a weary breath. No matter how conniving Adam Kember had been, Stephanie had been all set to elope with him. As Dan had said, she wasn't exactly blameless.

"I guess we should make our calls," she said wearily, pushing the phone on the counter toward him. "You can use this phone. I'll call Stephanie's parents from my office."

She was too drained to talk long with the Glynns. Yawning, she set down her empty cup of coffee, turned off the light and locked her office. The main office was empty, as well. She wondered if Dan had left without saying goodbye.

He hadn't. Opening the door, she discovered him sitting on the front porch, gazing into the distance.

At the sound of her footsteps on the porch, he sprang to his feet. Rebecca locked the front door, then turned to him.

"Are you all right?" he asked.

He sounded so earnest, so sweetly concerned, she had to force herself to remember he'd been the mastermind of the shoe stunt that had so vexed her. How could she have been bothered by such a trivial bit of goofiness when such awful things, like unmanageable campers, lay waiting to trip her up?

The full impact of the night's potential for tragedy deluged her. The tears she'd been suppressing all night spilled over now. "Oh, Dan," she sobbed quietly, covering her face with her hands.

He closed his arms around her, held her, let her weep. "It's okay," he murmured. "It was a rough one. Go ahead and let it out."

She shuddered, released a watery sigh and pulled back. Slipping his arm around her, he ushered her down the steps and across the grass to the path that led back to her cabin.

"I'm such a wimp," she sighed, swabbing the lingering dampness from her cheeks.

"No, you're not."

"Calling Adam a little rat—"

"You're right," Dan assured her. "He *is* a little rat."

"If he is, then Stephanie is, too. They're both rats."

"And they're both safe and sound."

"And I'm crying like an idiot," she said, sniffling.

"You're allowed," he told her, catching a teardrop at the tip of her chin. "You've never been through anything like this before. Spend a few years running a summer camp, and you'll get used to this sort of thing."

"Really? Have you gone through nonsense like this before?"

He guided her in front of him when the path narrowed, keeping his hand comfortingly on her shoulder as they wove through the woods to her cabin. "Last summer I had a kid who harassed a raccoon so badly, the poor creature bit him. The summer before that, we had a near drowning."

"Dear Lord," she sighed.

"If the boy had drowned, I would have been devastated. But he didn't. He came back to Mohawk last summer, and again this summer. Just last week he got his Red Cross intermediate swimmer's card. He's a great kid." They had reached her cabin, and he stopped beside the bottom step outside the door. "You've got to do the best you can, and that's all. You can't let a disaster knock you over—you've got all those other campers depending on you to have a fun summer."

"Dan." She climbed up a step to her porch and turned so she could stand eye to eye with him. No matter what upheavals they'd gone through in the past, she owed him a great deal tonight. "I couldn't have gotten through this without you."

"Sure, you could have," he said modestly.

"No. You were amazing. You took charge, you handled everything, you kept your head...,"

"So did you."

"Only because you were with me. I needed you out there, Dan. I needed you to get me through it."

He took her hand in his. She looked down and saw his thick fingers laced through her slender ones, saw the contrast of his sun-darkened skin against her paler skin. Her words reverberated inside her.

I need you, she thought, raising her eyes as he leaned toward her, as he slid his hand under her chin and drew her lips to his.

Chapter Thirteen

They lay facing each other on her narrow cot, her bedside lamp turned low. He was deep inside her, motionless, savoring the silken warmth of her around him, the tiny shivers of sensation she imparted to him, the frenzied beat of her heart against his hand as he played his fingers lightly over her breast. Her eyes were half-closed, her breath shallow, her lips swollen from too many kisses.

Moaning softly, she arched her hips. "I can't..." she pleaded.

He drew his hand to her bottom and held her still. He wanted to stay like this as long as he could, but if she moved he wouldn't be able to. Every fiber in his body ached for release. The torment of holding back was unbearable—and unbearably wonderful. He wanted to see how long he could make it last.

She shifted again, moaned again, slid her hand down his side and forward, massaging him just above where their bodies were joined. "Please, Dan..."

His control dissolved. He raised himself above her, pressed her down into the thin mattress and thrust hard, reaching for her again and again. If he were thinking lucidly, he would have to marvel at the power of this woman to make him want so much, so much of her. Not just her body, but everything. He wanted everything.

Her hands fisted against his back; her legs rose to circle his hips. He gazed down into her face and saw in it a reflection of the tension in her body, the ecstasy, the desperate yearning. She closed her eyes, bit her lip, turned her head and rose to meet him in a final, ravaging surge. Her body contracted around him, undulated, milked him until he exploded in an excruciating burst of ecstasy.

He bowed and touched his mouth to hers. Her eyes fluttered open, her pale golden lashes catching the light as her lips softened against his. When he drew back, she gave him a smile of utter contentment.

He was content, too, but... No use denying it. He wanted more.

"Dan." She lifted her hand to his hair, wove her fingers through the tangled mane and brushed it back from his face. "I really have to thank you."

"I think you just did," he said, mirroring her smile.

She sighed happily, threading her fingers through his hair again. They felt cool against his cheek, against his ear. "What I mean is, I have to thank you for helping me let go."

"It's all a matter of technique," he boasted.

She pulled a face and pretended she was going to slap him. He grasped her wrist and pressed her palm to his lips. Sighing again, she curled her fingers around his thumb and pulled his hand down to rest in the hollow between her breasts. "Listen to me, will you? I'm saying something nice about you, so don't interrupt."

"Go ahead. Say something nice." *Tell me you love me. Tell me you're mine.*

"I've never . . . I've never been really good at having fun. I mean, I've enjoyed things, but just letting go and having fun . . ." She drifted off for a moment, apparently searching for the right words. "I was raised in a very serious, businesslike environment, where everyone's future was mapped out and we all knew exactly what we were supposed to do. When I went to Maine, or to North Carolina—it was viewed as out of line, a wasted step. No one ever thought that maybe these were just things I wanted to do. Sometimes even *I* didn't think that. Do you understand what I'm saying?"

"Not really," he admitted.

His candor brought a smile to her lips. "I never did anything just for the fun of it. Some things turned out to be fun anyway, but that wasn't why I did them. Until now."

"I'm glad you thought this was fun." Personally he'd thought it was phenomenal, but this didn't seem like the right time to argue semantics with her.

"I was so upset about what happened with Adam and Stephanie, and yet when it was all over I was afraid to let out all my pent-up emotions. You said it was all right to cry—and I felt so much better afterward."

He still wasn't sure what she was getting at, but he was thrilled that she was sharing her private thoughts with him. "I think it was the past ten minutes that made you feel better," he suggested. "I feel kind of terrific myself."

"It's not just the sex," she said. "It's letting go. It's not attaching so much importance to everything I do. I've finally come to see that I don't have to take everything so seriously all the time. I've learned that from you. And I appreciate it."

Dan was beginning to understand. He should have been gratified, but he wasn't. Over the past week—and particularly over the past several minutes—he had been learning about his own capacity for taking things seriously. Not everything, but some things.

Like Rebecca. Like the fact that he couldn't stop thinking about her and dreaming about her. Like the way she made him crazy with anger and with lust, the way she aroused in him the desire not just to make love to her but to comfort and protect her. Like his admiration for her strength and, even though it exasperated him, her stubbornness.

Like the fact that the moment he went slack and his body slipped free of hers, he'd felt absurdly, inexplicably lonesome.

"So," he said in a falsely bright tone, "exactly what is it you don't take seriously?"

"Well, of course I take my job seriously, and the welfare of my campers, and all my responsibilities here at Chippewa. Girls who run away from camp with their boyfriends—I take that seriously. But the rest... I want to have fun, Dan. I want to have fun with you. I want to go camping and swimming and roast marshmallows and sing folk songs because it's fun. I want to pig out on dough-boys and be passionate and beat the pants off you and your Hawks at the water Olympics—just for the fun of it.''

''I like the part about beating the pants off me,'' he said with a smile. But he wasn't feeling particularly elated.

''I thought I would have to stay away from men because I was confused about what I needed in a relationship,'' she went on, oblivious to his mood. ''I know what I need right now—just to relax and take myself a little less seriously.''

What about the future? he wanted to scream. What about the long view? What about her desire for children? What about growing up?

He had spent the past five days in a state of emotional chaos over Rebecca. He'd been enraged by her fuddy-duddy response to the clothesline-shoes caper, and enraged with himself for giving a damn about what she thought of him. He'd been infuriated by her unshakable hold on his imagination. He'd been frustrated and irritable—and then, gradually, philosophical.

He'd thought about how, as he grew older, his needs and goals were evolving. He'd thought about his good pal Chuck, who hadn't had to cope with a damaged heart alone. Chuck had Irene. They were united, backing each other up, pushing each other forward. Loving each other. Renewing their commitment every day.

More than fun—that was what Dan wanted.

With Rebecca.

As he'd traipsed with her through the woods in search of their missing campers, he'd felt even more sure of what he wanted. He'd liked the way they'd been a team, shouldering their obligations together, handling their potential disaster in a seamless collaboration. Afterward, when she'd given in to tears, he'd liked the way she'd leaned on him.

He traced her nose with the tip of his index finger, the curve of her lower lip, her exquisitely chiseled cheekbones. "I hate to spoil the mood, Becky," he murmured, apprehensive about how she'd react, "but I think there's a lot more than fun going on here."

Her eyes sharpened on him, shimmering enigmatically. "What do you mean?"

"You know what I mean," he said. He didn't want to have to put his feelings into words; he didn't even know what words to use. But her perplexed gaze compelled him to try. "I mean...something that goes beyond August."

Her wide-eyed silence vexed him. He had hoped she would wrap him in a big hug and say, "Yes! I agree!" Or even, "I'm not sure. Convince me." By saying nothing, though, she forced him to keep talking.

"I care about you. I don't know if I can think of this as a summer romp anymore."

At last she looked away. Her eyes glistened with moisture, and she pressed her knuckles to her mouth. After an agonizing minute, she said, "I can't think beyond August, Dan. Please don't ask me to."

White-hot rage flashed through him, scorching everything in its path and leaving a bleak desert in its wake. "All right," he snapped, shoving himself up to sit and reaching for his jeans, which lay discarded on the floor beside the bed. "Forget it. Forget I said anything."

"Dan—" She reached for him, her fingers stroking his back, sparking a fresh paroxysm of outrage that she could turn him on even when he was busy despising her. He jerked away from her and hustled into his underwear.

"Dan," she said again, sitting up and reaching around to hug him from behind. The sight of her hands meeting above his navel, the feel of her cheek against his back... He cursed his body for responding.

"I'm not saying no," she murmured. "I care for you, too. A lot. But—it's summertime. Everything is a little unreal. We're both away from our homes, our regular lives, and..." She exhaled.

He refused to look at her. "And what?"

"At the end of August we're both going to leave Silver Lake. Who knows what might happen then?"

"You're right," he grumbled. "I might turn into a pumpkin. You might turn into Wallace's wife. The possibilities are endless."

"Listen to me. I'm trying to be logical. Everything's different here. The air is cleaner. The night is starrier. We've got wood fires and open skies and...it's all kind of magical. I've never felt this way before, and I don't know if I'll ever feel this way again."

"Well, I sure as hell won't count on it."

"Dan, please understand. I can't make any promises, not now. You said you wanted to have some sim-

ple summer fun, and it's taken me this long to see
things your way. You can't ask more of me.''

"Don't worry. I won't.''

"Can't we just enjoy the rest of the summer and
then see what happens?''

"I have every intention of enjoying the rest of the
summer,'' he assured her, his voice gritty with barely
contained fury. It didn't matter that she was saying
exactly what he'd been thinking when he'd first met
her, when he'd first tried to interest her in a summer
fling. It didn't matter that her words echoed with
honesty, that he couldn't refute them, that even if
what he was feeling for her right now was love, he
couldn't guarantee that he'd still be in love with her
once September arrived and he had to go back to the
real world.

All that mattered was that he'd presented her with
his soul and she'd turned him down.

He wrestled into his Camp Mohawk shirt, shoved
his feet into his hiking boots and pulled so hard on the
leather laces he gouged red welts into his fingers.
Standing, he reached for his wool overshirt and slung
it on. "See you around,'' he muttered, grabbing his
flashlight and stalking toward the door.

"Dan!'' She sprang off the bed, and he was stunned
by her daunting beauty. He remembered her bashfulness the first time he'd undressed her, by the campfire
on the bluff. Now she stood naked before him, all
creamy skin and feminine curves, her breasts round
and firm, her nipples taut and pink, her hips lean, her
thighs framing the pale, downy hair that veiled her
womanhood.

Fending off an acute tug of desire, he raised his eyes to her face. She held her chin high; her eyes cut into him, as silver as honed and polished steel. "I thought you didn't want anything more than this summer," she said. "I thought all you wanted was clean, healthy fun."

"Then I got what I wanted, didn't I?"

"And you're just going to leave?"

He struggled to breathe normally, to hold himself still, to withstand the very real urge to race back into her arms, into her bed.

He couldn't. He had offered Rebecca more than he'd thought himself capable of giving, and she'd refused to take it. He would never offer her anything again. Never.

"Yeah," he answered, turning and reaching for the doorknob. "I'm just going to leave."

THE BANG OF THE CABIN door slamming shut behind him reverberated inside her long after the room grew silent.

She grabbed one of her shoes and threw it at the door. Then she sank onto her bed and let a sob convulse her.

She wasn't going to cry, not for Dan Macklin. For her fugitive camper she would cry, but Dan didn't deserve her tears. He wasn't worth it.

What was wrong with him? Why, when she'd finally come around to seeing things his way, did he suddenly issue a whole new set of conditions? Was it his ambition in life to make her crazy?

Obviously. Right from the start he'd been playing head games with her, needling her, bedeviling her. Now that she'd finally accepted his idea of a romantic summer fling, he realized he couldn't get his kicks by hassling her anymore, so he'd changed his tack and his tactics.

Surely he couldn't be serious about wanting to get serious. Not the five-star general of the water brigade, not the scamp who taunted her at every opportunity. Not the man whose impassioned defense of summer fun had at long last won her over.

She wasn't going to weep for him, no way.

And if her bed still held his warmth? If her body still tingled and throbbed in the aftermath of his lovemaking? If closing her eyes filled her mind with the low, gravelly sound of his voice, the profound intimacy of his body inhabiting hers...

She would get over it. She had seen her campers and herself through a lot of ups and downs in the past few weeks. She could climb back up from this latest down.

For her own sanity, she would get over Dan Macklin.

THE MORNING OF THE water Olympics, Rebecca stepped out of her cabin to discover an ideal day—cloudless blue sky, warm sun, a light breeze, perfect weather for both swimming and boating.

She felt miserable.

Two weeks had passed since Dan had stormed out of her cabin. Two long, dismal, hot, sticky weeks. All around her Chippewa campers were having a grand time—she made sure of it—while their leader was suffering from a world-class case of the doldrums.

Dan hadn't attended the social at Camp Chippewa the previous Friday. She hadn't attended the social at Camp Mohawk the week before. She hadn't seen him, heard from him, received anything more than his perfunctory messages through Maggie regarding the final preparations for the Olympics. Rebecca had deliberately left Maggie in charge of all intercamp communications on the subject, and concentrated her own efforts on whipping the Chippies into shape, boosting their morale, exhorting them to win.

As if beating the pants off the manly men of Camp Mohawk was going to be even remotely fun.

"Are you ready for action?" Maggie asked as Rebecca approached her at the waterfront. The entire swimming area was festooned with banners and balloons—even an Olympics torch made of papier-mâché.

"I'm as ready as I'll ever be," she muttered. "We got nice weather, didn't we?"

"Thank goodness it's not another dog day. That week of hazy-hot-humid had us all dragging our feet."

If Rebecca had been dragging her feet, it wasn't due to August's dog days. But she saw no reason to correct Maggie. "I want our girls to win," she declared solemnly.

Maggie grinned as the Chippewa girls swarmed down the hill to the swimming area. Over their swimsuits they wore white sheets tied into togas, and construction-paper laurels adorned their hair. "So do the girls," she said. "I've never seen them so psyched before."

Turning back to the lake, Rebecca saw the first boats begin their journey west from Camp Mohawk.

"I'll go turn on the fanfare," Maggie said, sprinting across the beach to a boom box. She turned on the tape player, and a rendition of the familiar Olympics theme song resounded across the lake.

The festive atmosphere nearly overcame Rebecca's dark mood. She rotated back to the lake, and her gloom returned at the sight of the invading Mohawks. The boys were dressed as Native Americans, complete with paper headdresses and war paint.

She didn't want to scour the advancing hordes in search of their leader, but she couldn't help herself. Every time she spotted an adult in one of the boats, she squinted to see if it was Dan. It was always someone else, though, a counselor or staffer.

She knew he had to be in one of the boats. While he'd been within his rights to stay home during a social, he couldn't sit out the annual intercamp water Olympics. No matter how much he despised Rebecca, he had to come to Chippewa today.

Finally she located him in one of the last canoes. He stroked smoothly and swiftly through the water, his prow pointed like a missile at Chippewa's dock. He had on a majestic beaded and feathered war bonnet. Like his campers, he wore a green Camp Mohawk T-shirt, but even at a distance Rebecca could imagine the magnificent contours of his chest. The way he gripped the end of his paddle reminded her of the strength and grace of his hands as they'd curved around her breast, as he'd brushed the thick ridge of his knuckles along her jawline, as he'd clasped her hips and pulled her to himself. . . .

Swallowing, she turned away.

The first wave of Mohawks was disembarking, whooping and prancing across the beach. Shedding their togas and laurels, the girls of Chippewa shrieked and snickered at their competitors. The boys shrieked and snickered right back. Rebecca tried to sort the girls into their cabin groupings, but they merely swirled around her, disregarding her pleas for order.

"Hey, everybody, chill out!" came a deep, husky, excessively masculine voice behind her. Sucking in a deep breath, Rebecca rotated to confront Dan Macklin.

He ought to have looked ridiculous in his war bonnet and face paint. He didn't. The stripes of red and black streaking his face emphasized its strong, hard lines. The headdress, while flamboyant, reminded Rebecca of other feathers, other times with him, other, warmer feelings.

Which wasn't to imply that she didn't feel warm right now. In fact, she felt uncomfortably hot, feverish, flushed with embarrassment and discomfort and an irrepressible yearning to embrace him.

No. She didn't want anything even remotely personal to do with him. "Welcome to the water Olympics," she said cordially, wondering if anyone besides herself could hear the quiver in her voice.

"Welcome to your doom," Dan responded amid hoots from his Mohawks.

His melodramatic warning was the sweetest consolation she could imagine. He was clearly determined to maintain a light, professional attitude. All remnants of their last meeting—the passion, the honesty, the pain of it—would remain locked away, out of reach. Today was for fun—the campers' fun.

She sent him a small, meaningful smile of thanks. "Prepare to be disappointed," she shot back, then turned to her girls. "Come on, Chippewa—let's teach these little boys something about sportswomanship!"

With that, the games began. On the deep-water side of the dock, swimming races were organized; on the shallow side, less-skilled swimmers engaged in other types of competition; while on the beach, two artisans, one chosen from each camp, began the sandcastle construction contest.

While Rebecca remained occupied on the shallow end, Dan monitored the deep-water contests. Whenever she could, she glanced toward the deep water, telling herself she was concerned about the performance of her senior campers. This year, it seemed, the girls were no longer deliberately letting the boys win. Each girl threw herself into the competition, regardless of whether or not the boys would like her when she won.

Between the longest-back-float contest and the rock-skipping contest—"The Hawks *own* that one," Maggie had rightly warned—Rebecca wandered down to one end of the deep-water section to watch her older girls race out to the raft and back. She spotted Stephanie Glynn, looking appealingly unglamorous, her hair pulled back into a simple ponytail and her towel slung haphazardly around her shoulders as she yelled words of encouragement to one of the other girls, who was putting her all into a backstroke relay.

"How are we doing?" Rebecca asked.

"They're losers," Stephanie replied, hoarse from screaming but obviously proud of her teammates' swimming. "Boys are such dirtballs. I mean, really, like, if it wasn't so much fun to beat them in races, I wouldn't want anything to do with them at all."

Smiling at Stephanie's insight, Rebecca gazed across the lanes of racers and saw Dan standing on the other end of the dock. He had removed his headdress—all the Mohawks had—and his face shimmered with sweat in the hot sun. She lowered her gaze to his long, athletic legs, bare beneath the midthigh hems of his swim trunks, his muscular calves webbed with a fine covering of dark hair.

Stephanie thought beating boys at races was fun. And it was—but it was more than just fun. Winning gave the Chippewas a sense of their own power, an understanding of their own strength and ambition. It had nothing to do with their wardrobes or their complexions or how many earrings they had dangling from each lobe. It had to do with fearlessness and courage and letting go.

Just like making love, Rebecca thought. She'd thought the moments she spent in Dan's arms had been fun, and they had been. But as she studied him from across the dock, as she took in the leonine length of his wild dark hair, the sleek musculature of his torso, his hard biceps and bony wrists, she understood how similar making love with him had been to the exhilaration her campers were enjoying as they threw themselves into the competition.

She had been fearless with Dan, brave and free. If only he'd given her a little more time to figure out what was important, if only he hadn't rushed her and then retreated from his own tenuous promises. . . .

If only, if only. He'd done what he did because he was who he was: a man who panicked like a little boy, running for his life the moment a woman showed some spunk.

The Mohawk competitor finished his lap and tagged the next member of his relay team. Dan shouted something to the swimmer diving in, then glanced up and caught Rebecca staring at him. She fought the temptation to look away.

His eyes were a mesmerizing blend of color, green like the fir trees bordering the lake and blue like the clear August sky. They seemed to convey some message, but Rebecca couldn't decipher it. He was smiling, yet there was something rueful in his expression, something pensive. Perhaps he sensed, as she did, that no matter how many winners emerged from the day's Olympics, he and Rebecca had lost something forever.

The day wore on. Wins and losses were posted, sandwiches devoured, insults traded. The Hawk who'd spent the past several socials attached to Torie Schwartz tried to steal a kiss, and she slapped him away, saying, "We're enemies today. Keep your distance, dude."

Rebecca grinned, but she felt a stab of pain inside. She and Dan were enemies today, too. They were consummate professionals, moving the games along, inspiring their teams—but their enmity wouldn't vanish the moment the final score was posted. If anything, it would deepen—because then there would no longer be any Olympics rivalry between them. They would lose their shields of professionalism and loathe each other for personal reasons.

And as she watched her campers having the most exuberant, exciting water Olympics in the history of Camp Chippewa, something inside her died a slow, sad death.

"This is it," Maggie proclaimed through the megaphone as the tallies were announced at around three-thirty that afternoon. "We're all tied up! The final event—the canoe swamping—will determine the winner. Mohawk and Chippewa teams, please step forward!"

Rebecca joined the rest of her campers in shouting encouragements to the Chippewa team—four boats in all, each with one girl paddling in the stern and one girl armed with a bucket in the front. They paddled out into the deeper water, where they met up with the Mohawk team.

Maggie raised the megaphone. "On your marks, get set, go!"

The girls filled their buckets with water and dumped them as best they could into the boys' canoes, while the boys attempted to do the same. The paddlers worked furiously to maneuver their vessels; when they weren't trying to flood their opponents' boats, the bucket wielders attempted to bail out their own boats.

Along the shore the cheers of the Mohawks and Chippewas reached a breathtaking pitch. Rebecca let their spirit infuse her. She didn't want to notice the last flicker of love for Dan guttering in her soul. If she shouted loudly enough, she could ignore her sorrow for a while.

She stood among her campers, roaring, jumping up and down. This might be the only win of her summer, and she wanted it with all her heart.

"Go in," someone near Rebecca yelled when each team lost one canoe. "Come on, Rebecca—go in!"

She turned and frowned. "What?"

"Take a canoe for Chippewa! Dan Macklin is getting one."

She scanned the shoreline and saw him being pushed by his campers toward an empty canoe. Before she could object, Kelly thrust a bucket into her hands. "Go," Kelly urged her. "Win one for the Chippers!"

Rebecca let them push her into an empty canoe. Shaking off her momentary surprise, she tightened her grip on the paddle and steered around the swimming dock, out toward the other canoes. Out toward Dan's canoe.

He looked somber and somewhat reluctant as he glided toward her. She sent him a bittersweet smile. He returned it, shrugged, then scooped a bucketful of water out of the lake and flung it at her, laughing maliciously as the water struck its target.

She screamed as the cold water hit her. "Win one for the Chippers!" the girls on shore hollered. Rebecca would win one, for them and for herself and for all the women of the world who were sick and tired of men and their silly games, all the women who'd ever opened their hearts and been wounded.

She filled her bucket and hurled it directly at Dan Macklin's smug grin.

Sputtering, he paddled backward. She advanced. He dumped a bucket of water into her boat. She heaved a bucket of water at his chest.

This wasn't a competition; it was war. It wasn't Camp Chippewa versus Camp Mohawk; it was Rebecca versus Dan. She lost track of the competing campers; her attention was focused solely on her foe.

Dan was stronger and more skilled than she, but he made one mistake: he neglected to bail out his boat as he continued his assault on hers. Rebecca ignored the bobbing and twisting of her canoe; she propped her paddle between her knees and used both hands to fill the bucket and dump, fill and dump.

His canoe sank lower.

"I'm going to get you!" he boasted.

"You're all wet, Macklin!"

"You're weak!"

"You're going down!"

He paddled close, pulled his canoe alongside hers and raised a full bucket in both hands. She grabbed the edge of his boat and gave it a shake. The bucket slipped and emptied its contents onto him.

He cursed, then laughed. Joining his laughter, Rebecca dumped another bucket of water into his boat— and watched with unabashed glee as it submerged fully.

"I'll get you!" he shouted an instant before his canoe rolled onto its side and threw him into the lake.

A triumphant chorus of cheers arose from the Chippewa end of the beach, but Rebecca barely heard it. She stared only at Dan's empty canoe, which had righted itself. She stared at the abandoned bucket and paddle floating in a couple of inches of water at the bottom of the canoe, and then at the trailing stream of bubbles where Dan had plunged into the water, and then at the stillness.

Something was wrong. He hadn't surfaced. Maybe he'd hit his head, maybe he'd gotten a cramp—something was wrong!

She rose high on her knees and leaned over the edge of her canoe, searching the still, dark water for a sign of him. Suddenly she felt a billowing motion beneath her, pushing, tilting. Her canoe rocked up on the far side, rose out of the water and overturned.

The lake swallowed her scream. She kicked free of the boat and felt an arm circling her waist, pulling her away. Dragging her against himself, Dan lifted her up toward the sky with powerful kicks and strokes.

They surfaced together, gasping and gulping in lungfuls of air. The sun felt hot against her cheeks and shoulders—and then she realized it was Dan heating her blood, his arms still tight around her waist, his legs weaving between hers as he treaded water, his face less than an inch from hers.

She wanted to kiss him. More than she'd ever wanted anything before. She wanted to wrap her arms around him and press her mouth to his and swear that she would be his long after August ended, long after the leaves turned color and fell and the ground froze into stone, and then thawed and sprouted new life and began the cycle once more, carrying them into another summer and another and on into eternity....

She wanted to promise him her future, her life. She wanted to take the longest view in the world and see him at the end of it, with his arms still tight around her.

A devilish smile spread his lips, and he let go of her. "Who's all wet now?" he taunted, swimming from her in long, robust strokes.

Too stunned to move, she sank until the water closed above her head. She hastily propelled herself back to the surface, blinking the moisture from her eyes and assuring herself it wasn't tears.

In a minute she would recover enough to swim to shore. But for now all she could think of was the way she'd felt in Dan's arms, the way her heart had opened to him—and the way he'd swum from her. His final words echoed inside her, mocking, insinuating, downright cruel.

And then she recalled the first words he'd spoken to her that day: *Welcome to your doom.*

She wasn't going to go under. She wasn't going to struggle for breath or strain to reach the shore. She was a good swimmer; she'd make it back to shore without any difficulty.

But even after she was back on terra firma, wrapped in a towel and accepting the congratulations of her campers for having swamped Dan's canoe, her soul would resonate with the understanding that in some profound way she had met her doom.

Chapter Fourteen

The sky above the eastern shore of Silver Lake had faded to lilac. The air smelled of pine smoke. It was an autumn scent, Rebecca thought wistfully, the aroma of cooler weather, of summer's end.

The haunting melody of "Kumbayah" echoed softly in her mind as she stirred the glowing embers left by the bonfire. Even the girls seemed mellow, content to bask in the glow of the fire and in the equally warm glow of their victory.

Maybe it wasn't fatigue from the Olympics that had made the final campfire more subdued than usual. Maybe it was the understanding that in a very short while the girls would be packing their trunks, donning their Chippewa sailor hats for the last time and bidding each other farewell for the winter.

Rebecca wondered whether her campers felt as ambivalent about leaving as she did.

She cast her gaze toward the eastern shore again. Graceful curls of black smoke rose from a dying campfire across the lake. Did the Hawks feel melancholy about the end of summer?

Turning her back on Camp Mohawk, she spotted a solitary figure perched on a boulder overlooking the swimming dock. Setting down the stick she'd been using to stir the embers, she walked over to the camper, who sat with her legs drawn up, her chin resting on her knees and her hands folded around her ankles. Her dark hair blew gently in the breeze rising off the lake, and her eyes shimmered with tears.

"Are you okay?" Rebecca asked.

Stephanie Glynn sniffled and nodded. "Yeah."

"It's kind of sad when camp winds down."

Stephanie nodded again.

Rebecca leaned her hips against the boulder next to Stephanie. "You swam really well today. I didn't know you were so strong in the butterfly."

"Yeah, well . . ." Stephanie shrugged and sniffled some more.

Rebecca dug a tissue out of her pocket and handed it to Stephanie. "Did you have fun today?"

"Yeah." She blew her nose loudly. "Thanks for not kicking me out of camp when I ran away."

Rebecca thought of a dozen responses—lectures on safety, the necessity for rules, the dangers faced by runaways—but opted for a simple, "You're welcome."

"He was such a creep, you know? He had such an attitude. He thought he was God's gift, just because he happened to be good-looking. I mean, really, who needs that?"

This time Rebecca couldn't think of a single response. She only nodded in sympathy.

"Trouble is..." Stephanie's voice broke, and she dabbed the crumpled tissue to her eyes and nose again. "I still do love him, sort of."

Rebecca longed to tell Stephanie she should forget Adam Kember. He had lured her into the woods on a dark night, devoured all the candy and then accused her of having a fat rear end. How could any girl, no matter how young and inexperienced, love a jerk like that?

How could any woman love a man who couldn't take anything seriously until he'd convinced the woman not to take him seriously, and then, when he'd experienced a change of heart, refused her the time she needed to adjust? How could a woman love a man when she wasn't sure where he was coming from, where he was going, what he wanted or how he intended to get it—in fact, when she wasn't sure of anything except that *he* wasn't sure of anything, either?

How could a woman love such a man?

"In time," she told Stephanie, "you'll remember Adam as your first love, and it will just be a nice, nostalgic memory, nothing more. You'll remember him and smile a little, and maybe cry a little, but you'll move on and meet other guys. Adam Kember is like a big bonfire inside you now, but eventually he'll burn down to an ember and then to ashes and a wisp of smoke."

Stephanie considered Rebecca's prediction. "And then he'll be gone?"

"Just a distant memory."

"And thinking about him won't hurt anymore?"

"You'll have other boys to think about."

Stephanie mulled over Rebecca's prediction and attempted a teary smile. ''I guess it's almost lights-out, huh.''

Rebecca patted her shoulder and helped her down from the boulder. ''Sleep tight, Stephanie.''

Alone, she took Stephanie's place on the boulder and surveyed the lake. The sky above Camp Mohawk had darkened to a royal blue tinged with violet. If the fire there was still smoking, she could no longer see it.

Stephanie would get over Adam. Rebecca had no doubt of it. As for her own memories, her own feelings . . . she doubted they would burn to ash and blow away. Dan Macklin would remain with her forever, hot and smoldering. He would remain with her no matter how many other men she met, no matter whether she found a suitable partner, someone to marry and raise children with. Dan would always be there.

What if she climbed into a boat right now and rowed across the lake? What if she raced through Camp Mohawk until she found him, and said, ''Yes, I want to be serious with you and take the long view''?

If she did, he would no doubt smirk and say, ''Who's all wet now?''

He'd pulled the ultimate practical joke, hadn't he? He'd built her up, made lofty claims, convinced her he was serious and then, when she was prepared to recognize the enormity of their love, he'd resorted to his lighthearted teasing and deflated her like an air-filled doll.

It had all been just another gag. Dan Macklin didn't know how to get serious about anything.

I survived Camp Chippewa—barely, she thought, her eyes misting. She dug into her pockets and found she'd given Stephanie her last tissue. Well, that solved that problem—without a decent supply of tissues, she wasn't about to start crying.

What she would have to do instead was regain control. She would stop taking chances. She would force her life back into a manageable shape, and return to New York and her family and her job at Claremont. She could marry a proper gentleman and raise a family, or stay single and never have children—or, maybe, stay single and adopt a child. She could work that out later, when she was ready to take the long view.

The short view was that she would survive. With luck the fire raging inside her would subside until it was nothing more than the glowing embers she'd been trying to extinguish just minutes ago. She would cool off, gather herself up, hold herself in and never let go.

DAN GAZED AROUND him with a sense of unreality. The final car had just driven through the main gate in a cloud of dust, carrying away the last of the Hawks. Other than a skeleton maintenance crew, Camp Mohawk was vacant.

His sneakers crunched against the loose gravel as he strode across the empty lot and into the woods. Closing the camp down entailed a great deal of work, but Dan had something more important to take care of first. He stalked through the woods to the administration building, into his office, to his desk. Slouching in his chair, he reached for the telephone and punched the buttons for Camp Chippewa.

Maggie Tyrell answered.

Dan greeted her, pretending he didn't feel as if his eternal fate rested on this one phone call. "Is Pruitt there?"

"Rebecca? No, she left."

"What do you mean, she left?" Camp Chippewa had as elaborate a closing-up procedure as Camp Mohawk did. Dan knew; he and Chuck had been through it together many times. During the last three days of August each summer, they had toiled all day and met for beers and griping every evening. Dan had assumed that, with the Chippies and Hawks no longer around, he and Rebecca could use these three days to talk things through and work things out. To discover a way to greet September together.

The possibility of Rebecca's leaving Silver Lake early had never occurred to him.

"How could she leave?" he protested. "She's got to shut the camp down."

"Artie Birnbaum came up to do it," Maggie explained. "Rebecca told Artie she wouldn't be able to stay through the last weekend in August. Apparently she's got to prepare for the school term at Claremont starting next week, and she wanted a weekend to decompress. So she's gone."

Gone. The word smacked into him with blunt force. "Where did she go? Back to New York?"

"I guess."

His first thought was to drive down to the city after her. But he couldn't do that, not when he had so much to attend to at Mohawk. "She didn't by any chance leave behind any messages, did she?'' he asked, already knowing the answer.

''Nope. She didn't even gloat about our big Olympics win. I had to call Chuck DeVore with the news.''

''It probably gave him another heart attack.''

''He said it was about time you got your butt kicked,'' Maggie quoted. ''Listen, Danny, I've got a million things to do here. Is there anything Artie or I can help you out with?''

''No, thanks.''

''You want Rebecca's phone number in New York?''

Dan hesitated. He couldn't call her there, not when she'd so clearly cut herself off from him. ''No, that's all right,'' he said, priding himself on his ability to accept the truth without flying into a rage and smashing things. After saying goodbye, he lowered the phone gently into its cradle.

He swiveled his chair to face the window. Through the trees he saw the winking blue of the lake.

She was gone. Back to the real world, the world she didn't believe held a future for them. Back to the world of prep-school girls and their trust funds. The world of her father and his charming new *très magnifique* bistro on Madison Avenue. The world of a Wall Street broker who could provide her with a roof over her head, even though Dan knew—and Rebecca knew, too—that a night sky scattered with stars was better than the best roof ever built.

Dan had wanted a summer fling, and Rebecca had fulfilled his wish. But then he'd gotten greedy and wanted more.

And now she was gone. August was gone. The magic was gone.

Unable to endure the sight of Camp Chippewa any longer, he turned back to his office. He stared at the file cabinets, the spiderweb near the ceiling, the dust on the floor. Half-buried in the dust was a small white fuzz of some sort. Frowning, Dan went to pick up the white tuft from the floor. It was a feather from a pillow.

He cursed. Straightening up, he kicked it back into the corner with the dust and then headed for the door. An entire camp required his attention. It was time to put the summer away.

"No, MOM," REBECCA SAID into the phone. "I can't, okay? I just can't."

"I don't mean to pressure you, Rebecca. But you know how happy we are that you're finally back. Please come for dinner. We want you with us."

Rebecca had been with her family—physically— ever since she'd driven into New York City Friday afternoon. But emotionally she was far away. She doubted she would ever be "back," not the way her family wanted her to be back.

Yet she wasn't where she wanted to be, either. She'd left her old place, turned away from it, moved on. She hadn't arrived anywhere, though. All she knew was that her heart was reading a different compass than her head, and its needle pointed to a destination she didn't think she would ever reach.

From the moment she'd found a parking space on the picturesque Upper West Side block of well-preserved brownstones abutting Central Park, her family had swooped down and taken over her life. Rebecca hadn't even unpacked before her sister was dragging her across town to Maurice's for a proper haircut. From there she had been hustled over to her parents' East Side town house, where her mother had thrown together a "casual" dinner for twenty. Rebecca had had to smile and make polite chit-chat with Aunt Gert and Cousin Randolph and the Haverhills. She'd had to nibble on capon stuffed with wild rice and endive salad while her father pontificated on the wine and Lisbeth Haverhill said things like, "Did you really sleep in the dirt at that spa?"

"It wasn't a spa, it was a summer camp," Rebecca had answered, "and the general practice was to sleep inside a sleeping bag, not directly in the dirt."

"However does one maintain one's manicure in such a life-style?"

"It wasn't a life-style," Rebecca explained as courteously as possible. "It was a summer camp."

She'd gone home shortly after dinner, washed all of Maurice's styling additives out of her hair and collapsed into bed. The superfirm posture-perfect mattress felt strange after a summer on her sagging cot at Chippewa. The sheets felt too smooth and crisp. The air smelled dead.

Unable to sleep, she'd rummaged through her closets until she found a pine-scented cleanser. She'd opened the bottle, taken a whiff and gagged. It smelled nothing like the clean, fresh pine of live trees standing tall, scraping their pointed green tips against the sky.

Capping the bottle, she'd found herself fighting the urge to weep. She didn't want to be in the city, listening to the sounds of speeding cabs and rumbling buses through her windows. She didn't want to look around her and see four plastered, painted walls hung with high-quality prints of Brueghel peasant scenes. She didn't want to walk on a hardwood floor covered with a plush Bellestan rug. She didn't want to live behind a two-inch-thick steel-reinforced door with a knob lock, a dead bolt and a chain strung across it.

Before this summer, city living hadn't bothered her. But something had happened in the past several weeks. Something had altered her in such a way that escaping to the wilderness was no longer a rebellion or a retreat. It was something she truly *wanted* to do, just for fun.

Something had happened to her, and his name was Daniel Macklin.

And she'd walked away from him, because she didn't honestly believe he knew how to be serious—or maybe because she was afraid that if he *did* know how to be serious she would relinquish her heart, her soul, her very existence to him. If Dan had turned out to be everything she needed and wanted, she would have to let go, forever.

She'd left Silver Lake because she'd been scared. Now she was in Manhattan, aching with loneliness—and just as scared.

She spent the entire weekend restless and melancholy. On Saturday her brother and his wife insisted on taking her to brunch at a trendy place where the menu described every dish in breathless detail. Afterward, Lisbeth Haverhill insisted on taking her to a manicurist. After an hour of Lisbeth's manicurist clucking over Rebecca's tragically neglected cuticles, Rebecca's mother insisted that she come over for an intimate family dinner. Intimate, Rebecca discovered, meant Spode china, Waterford crystal, Royal Doulton silverware and Wallace.

"I thought you were dating with Gwen Veebeck," Rebecca had commented once her parents left her and Wallace alone.

"Well...I am," he admitted, fussing with the cuffs of his spotless Ralph Lauren shirt. "She's a fine lady. I'm quite fond of her."

"I'm happy to hear it."

"That doesn't mean you and I can't reconsider our engagement," he pointed out.

"It doesn't?"

"We make a better couple, Rebecca. Gwen is horsey, you know. She's always riding. She doesn't want children—she thinks she won't be able to ride if she's pregnant."

"In other words, you want to marry me because I'm willing to spend nine months off a horse?"

"Don't be crass, Rebecca. I want to marry you because you're sensible and practical. You're willing to make the sacrifices necessary to be a mother. Once you marry me, you'll settle down and do what's right."

"In other words, no camping. No leaving town. No capsizing a canoe."

Wallace appeared taken aback. "No canoes, period. Canoes are so plebeian. You weren't canoeing this summer, were you?"

"Go back to Gwen, Wallace," Rebecca urged him. "You'll have better luck whipping her into line than you'll ever have with me."

Later, pacing her darkened bedroom after a futile attempt to fall asleep, Rebecca reconsidered her discussion with Wallace. Of all the things troubling her, all the recent events that had capsized her life more profoundly than any canoe-swamping competition, saying goodbye to Wallace was the only thing she'd done that felt right.

Without bothering to turn on the light, she groped along in her closet's cluttered floor until she found her sleeping bag. Unrolling it, she discovered that a few residual pine needles had made the trip to New York with her.

She plucked them from the nylon fabric and left them on her dresser. Then she smoothed the bag down on the rug and stretched out across it. It smelled of the fertile earth, the mountain sky and the crisp, evergreen air of Silver Lake.

It smelled of Dan.

No, it didn't, she told herself, bolting upright. It couldn't. He'd shared the sleeping bag with her only once, one night. She'd used it several times since then.

But never as joyously.

Oh, God, she missed him. More accurately, she missed the man she'd wanted him to be, the man he never could be: Dan, as solid and mature as he'd been the night Adam and Stephanie had tried to elope. Dan, as playful as he'd been delivering a bouquet of peacock feathers to her door. Dan, as sexy as he'd been stretched out on this very sleeping bag next to her, with the flickering golden glow of the campfire dancing across his bare skin and his eyes bright with the satisfaction of knowing he'd satisfied her.

She missed him. But it was over; August was over. She had to keep moving, hoping that eventually, without Dan or anyone else at her side, she would figure out where she was going, where she belonged.

By the time Monday morning dawned, Rebecca had spent three days eating off civilized tableware and dabbing her lips on civilized linen napkins and pacing the floors of her civilized apartment. She could not recall experiencing a single moment of fun since her departure from the primitive world of Silver Lake.

On Tuesday the very civilized Claremont School for Girls would be opening its doors. Rebecca decided to go to the school Monday morning and get her office organized. If she threw herself into her work, she wouldn't have time to mope about how much she missed Camp Chippewa, and her cabin, and her campers and...

No. She couldn't think about him anymore. Like the summer, he was gone, past.

She put on a silk dress, a proper pearl necklace and matching earrings, stockings and neat leather pumps with one-inch heels. She brushed her newly cut hair so it lay straight and loose around her shoulders, and she added only a minimum of cosmetics to her face.

Just before she reached the door, her telephone rang; her mother wanted her to come for dinner. Rebecca refused. If she didn't spend the evening alone—preferably eating something straight out of the can—she would go crazy.

"We would love to have you, dear," her mother said.

"I appreciate the invitation, Mom, but really, I'm going to be setting up my office at Claremont today. I'll be on the go all day. I need a night off."

Her mother paused. "You seem troubled, Rebecca."

"I am," she let slip, then sighed.

"Is it because of Wallace?"

"It's because of me. I've got a lot of things to work out, and I need some time alone to do that. Please try to understand."

Another pause, and then her mother said, "Do what's right for you, dear. You'll never be happy otherwise."

Astonished by her mother's unexpected show of sympathy, Rebecca felt her eyes well up. "Thank you for understanding," she murmured.

She repeated her mother's words silently as she hung up the phone, tucked her envelope purse under her arm and left her apartment. What if she *couldn't* do what was right for her? Would that mean she would never be happy?

She had to find Dan. It was as simple as that. She had to find him, or she would never even know what was right for her.

Chuck DeVore might know where he lived. If he wouldn't reveal his whereabouts, she'd track Dan down at the school where he taught.

And then what would she say? That if it wasn't too late she would like to take the long view with him? That three days in the city convinced her that she'd rather be with him—even if his offer of a future was null and void? That she would be willing to take it one day at a time, no promises, no commitments, because she'd never felt like this before and she never would again, and even an ill-fated fling with Dan would be better than nothing?

What if she was too late? What if he had already embarked on a new affair? What if he was right this minute blowing up his life-size doll and leaving it outside the office of the pretty young math teacher who'd just joined the faculty?

She would call Chuck the minute she got to her office. The very instant.

She raced down the remaining few stairs, opened the locked inner door, hurried through the vestibule and shoved open the decorative leaded-glass outer door. At the top of the concrete steps leading down to the sidewalk, she froze.

A man had just turned the corner from Central Park West and was strolling toward her building. He was dressed in tailored trousers and a sport jacket, his dark hair neatly groomed and his loafers relatively unscuffed. Hovering on the top step, she observed his profile: the strong, defiant chin, the straight nose, the high forehead, his eyes flashing green and blue in the morning sunlight.

She clung to the sculpted brownstone railing to keep from running away.

Sure, she'd fantasized about tracking Dan down. But all that other stuff, about giving herself to him, no strings attached, no promises . . . had she really meant it? Was she truly ready to see him?

No.

But she didn't have much choice. His stride had slowed as he read the wrought-iron numerals of the building next door to hers. He continued past it, squinting in search of her building's numbers. Seeing her, he halted.

She took a deep breath and descended the steps to the sidewalk. For a long, tense minute they stared at each other. A cab cruised down the street, honking its horn. The Columbus Avenue bus wheezed in the distance; the chattering of two neighbors across the street rose and fell in the morning air.

"Hi," said Dan. He wasn't smiling.

She didn't trust her voice, so she refrained from saying anything. Instead, she continued to study him. His hair was definitely shorter, parted and neatly combed. His jacket was a classic navy blue, his slacks a pleated gray, his shirt white with a button-down collar and his necktie maroon with a white stripe. The knot was loose and the collar button undone, but under her intense scrutiny he quickly closed the button and adjusted the knot snugly against his throat.

"Don't," she said, reaching for his wrist. The moment her fingertips grazed his skin, she recoiled, embarrassed by the casual intimacy of her gesture. "It's too hot for a necktie."

He let his arms fall to his sides and gazed at her hand. A pigeon waddled toward them, then about-faced and flew off to join its friends in Central Park.

"You got a haircut," she said, then silently chastised herself. Why couldn't she say what she was really thinking: that she'd planned to hunt him down, that she would accept his terms, whatever they were—that she would accept them without even knowing what they were. That she'd been going quietly insane ever since she'd left Silver Lake. That she hadn't been able to sleep. That she'd been weepy and gloomy and lonelier than she'd ever thought possible.

"Irene DeVore trimmed it for me," he said, ruffling one hand through his shorn locks. "I drove down to Long Island to visit Chuck last night, and...um..." He drifted off, his lips curving in a faint smile.

"How is he feeling?"

"Better."

You say it, Rebecca silently begged him. *I'm a coward—you already know that. So you say it, Dan—say what needs to be said.*

"Irene told me I ought to clean up my act."

Rebecca shook her head. She didn't know what act he was talking about, or how it should be cleaned up. "Is getting a haircut cleaning up your act?"

"The truth is, Becky..." He tapped his toe against the bottom step of her building's front stairway. She had never seen him so nervous, so ill at ease. Yet why shouldn't he be ill at ease in this neighborhood of buildings and roadways and automobiles? This wasn't the woods; it wasn't a bluff above a lake. It wasn't a tent, a canoe, a campfire beneath the stars.

It was civilization with a vengeance. "Look, Rebecca," he finally erupted in a rush, as if he were trying to get something ghastly over with. "This is as clean as my act gets. I don't even own a suit."

She gave his outfit one final appraisal. "You look civilized," she said, undecided about whether that was good or bad.

"You look..." His gaze journeyed from her silk dress to her pearls, to her meticulously trimmed hair and polished nails. "Citified."

"I've gone too long without a dough-boy," she murmured, hearing a catch in her voice and wondering if Dan had heard it, too.

He swallowed. His eyes were blue—as blue as she'd been feeling ever since she'd left the mountains, ever since he had let go of her and swum away. Ever since he'd walked out of her cabin without a backward glance.

"Becky, I..." He gazed past her and struggled with his thoughts. Then he steered his beautiful eyes back to her and exhaled. "I wasn't going to come here. I refused to take your number when Maggie Tyrell tried to give it to me. I wasn't going to do this."

"But you did," Rebecca said, wondering whether he regretted it, whether he was about to turn and walk out of her life again.

"Because I..." Again he paused to mull over his words. "I went to visit Chuck and he said, 'See her.'"

"And Chuck's wife said, 'Get a haircut,'" Rebecca added, hoping a little levity would make this easier on them both.

"Now I'm seeing you, Rebecca, and..." He shook his head. "You were right. This is the real world. You look like a grown-up. I mean—God, you're wearing stockings! And high heels! Expensive-looking ones."

"Dan—"

"I should have listened to you. This is your real life. In your real life you're a sophisticated city lady in high-priced clothes."

"And I miss you," she blurted out, feeling her eyes fill with tears for the zillionth time since she'd driven out of the Camp Chippewa parking lot last Friday. "I miss camping, and I miss my Chippies and, God help me, I miss you."

As her words registered on him, she saw him thawing, his tension draining from him. He opened his arms and she practically fell into them in her eagerness to hold him, to feel him holding her. Wrapping her arms tightly around his waist, she tilted her head back as he bowed his forward. Their mouths met in a scorching reunion. Dan probed, nipped, sipped and sucked, his tongue filling her mouth in relentless, rhythmic surges that shocked her with their erotic power.

He drew back to catch his breath, then rested his forehead against hers. "Whatever you want," he murmured, his tone low and hoarse. "No demands, Becky, no pushing. I promise. Whatever you want…"

"I want fun," she said, only partly joking.

"That can be arranged." He slid one hand down to her derriere and traced the curve of her flesh, guiding her body against his. "Right now."

"We're in the middle of the street," she pointed out, trying to back away yet not really minding when he refused to relax his embrace.

"We're on the sidewalk, but who's arguing?"

"You are," she chided, then smiled and touched her lips to his. He tasted familiar and new. He tasted like love. Like Dan. Like summer, like everything she needed, everything she had dreamed of. "Dan..." she whispered. "I want more than fun. Whatever *you* want, that's what I want."

His eyes sparkled with mischief. "Well, now that you mention it, I think fun is a great idea."

"Serious fun," she clarified. The pressure of his hand on her as he guided her hips to his sent shivers of yearning deep into her. As much as she wanted to give in to the desire he was stoking within her, she had to make sure they were both viewing things in the same way. "August is over, Dan, and this *is* my real life. This is where I live, where I work."

"I know. I'm a teacher, Rebecca. I've got a real life, too."

"Can we be together in real life?" she asked, bracing herself for whatever answer he would give.

Except for the answer she got: a hard, demanding, breath-stealing kiss. "We can do whatever we damned well want, if we want it enough," he said when at last his mouth released hers.

"All I want is you."

"I want you, too," he murmured, brushing his lips over hers again, this time with heartbreaking tenderness. At last he loosened his hold on her. He traced the arc of her necklace, circling the iridescent beads with his fingertips. "I can't be a rich husband for you, Rebecca. I doubt I'll ever be able to give you pearls."

"I've already got pearls," she pointed out. Dan had given her so much, and he could give her so much more. Pearls seemed insignificant in comparison. "Can you give me children?" she asked.

A smile tickled his lips, and there was nothing hesitant or anxious in it. "That can also be arranged—but first we'll have to get undressed."

"Not on the sidewalk," she warned as his hand moved from her necklace to the top button of her dress.

He raised his eyes to hers again. "Call me a prissy sissy, but I think we ought to get married before we make babies."

"All right."

His smile faded. "Are you sure?"

"About getting serious and taking the long view? Yes. I want to marry you, Dan."

His hand rose from the neckline of her dress to her cheek. He traced her cheekbone with his thumb, then brushed her hair back from her temple, examining her face in search of evidence that she didn't mean what she'd said. He must have seen in her steady gaze that she'd meant every single word, because his smile returned, stronger than before. "Do we have to have a party at the Plaza, with invitations from Tiffany?"

"I'd rather have a party in a sleeping bag under the stars."

"If you want a diamond ring, it's going to have to be the itsy-bitsy schoolteacher model."

"I want you, Dan. That's all that matters."

He bowed to kiss her again, with greater gentleness but even more passion. "I did bring you something, actually." He let go of her, reached into a pocket of his blazer and pulled out a hinged box.

Puzzled, she took it and opened the lid. Inside was a pair of earrings made of peacock feathers, two soft, brilliantly colored plumes dangling from simple gold wires. "They're beautiful!" she sighed, remembering once again the bouquet of peacock feathers he'd given her. She'd been too mournful to take them with her when she left Camp Chippewa. For all she knew, they were still in her dresser drawer at the camp. But she no longer needed them. She had these.

She had Dan.

She plucked off her pearl earrings, handed them to him and donned the feather earrings, their turquoise shimmer reflected in Dan's eyes. "How do they look?"

"Very silly, if you want to know the truth."

"Good."

"They might look better if you weren't wearing anything else."

"Let's find out," she said, taking his hand and starting up the steps.

"Don't you have to go to work or something? I mean, the way you're dressed—"

"There's nothing at my office that can't wait," she said. "I can be just as mature and responsible as I have to be, Dan, but—"

"But not when your passionate nature is running the show."

"My nature isn't—"

He turned her in his arms and silenced her with another consuming kiss, one that simultaneously soothed and excited her. The fire had never died inside her. It had burned low, singeing her with the constant pain of what she'd almost lost. But now she had everything she had ever feared losing. And with his kisses Dan fanned the fire inside her to a brighter, hotter flame.

She kissed him back just as fiercely, just as wildly. When at last they separated, she was too breathless to speak.

Dan spoke instead. "Let's have fun," he murmured, sending her a seductive grin. "Let's have lots of clean, healthy fun."

"Let's," she whispered, mirroring his smile and leading him into the building.

H A R L E Q U I N
American Romance ®

ABOUT THE AUTHOR

For Judith Arnold, summer is synonymous with camp. From ages eight to eighteen, she spent every summer at camps, usually in the Catskill Mountains—just like Chippewa and Mohawk. ''It was a real wild time for me,'' she says. ''In fact, one of the incidents in this book actually happened to me.'' But she won't tell us which one!

Like Rebecca Pruitt, Judith herself spent one summer setting up a day camp on a Cherokee Indian reservation in North Carolina's Smoky Mountains, an experience she remembers fondly.

Now the mother of two active young sons—who attend day camp—she always schedules family vacations for the month of August, usually in and around New England, where she and her family make their home.

JACOR

COMING NEXT MONTH

#453 RAFE'S REVENGE by Anne Stuart

In Hollywood, where only winners survived, Rafe McGinnis was
known as a fighter who never gave up. And neither did film
critic Silver Carlysle. Theirs was a battle of wills—but each new
skirmish only fueled their mutual desire. Despite the danger,
Silver couldn't surrender. For Rafe had laid out his terms:
Nothing less than a night in her arms would satisfy him.

#454 ONCE UPON A TIME by Rebecca Flanders

With buccaneer blood in his veins and a savage thirst for
adventure, Chris Vandermere loomed like a modern-day pirate
to his sassy stowaway, Lanie Robinson. She thought such men
lived only in her dreams, but then she met Chris's lips and
fantasy threatened to become reality.

#455 SAND MAN by Tracy Hughes

Like the Sand Man of her childhood dreams, Jake Abel brought
a special magic into Maggie Conrad's life. Jake was anything
but a myth. When he sprinkled his magic dust, Maggie almost
believed that wishes could come true—despite their differences.
But Jake was unstoppable and he'd made up his mind. He
wanted Maggie in his life . . . and in his bed.

#456 THE COWBOY'S MISTRESS by Cathy Gillen Thacker

In the battle for the Bar W Ranch, Travis Wescott employed his
devilish, double-edged tongue—using one side for witty repartee
and the other for kissing his flame-haired adversary, Rachel. She
meant to show him no one could rein in her ambition. And now
Travis dreamed of claiming his ranch and branding Rachel
his forever.